Mission Earth

The Journey Home
By
Dan Robinson

This book is dedicated to my mother, Easter Diane Robinson. She was the light of my life for 64 years.

ISBN: 9798504824062

Table of Contents

"If we don't end war, war will end us,"
–H. G. Wells

Chapter 1

Earth - 2355

Rocky Mountains—Colorado

Hovering no more than a breath away from his hunting partner, Fred Jacobs whispered, "Ya see it?"

"Nope, but I'm pretty sure I heard it," Joe Titus murmured. Holding a finger to his lips, Titus, an expert with a bow, reached up to part a few branches, scanning the clearing beyond. The deer had bolted through that spot only a moment earlier. Thinking their prey was just on the other side, they crouched behind a thick clump of bushes, not wanting to spook it.

In a tone barely above a whisper, Titus said, "It couldn't have gone far. My steel-tipped shaft stuck in its left shoulder. I know it's gonna die, but it might take a while before it drops." He leaned in and peered through the opening. Suddenly, his body went rigid. "Dear God, no. No, no, no. It cain't be," he breathed, jerking back to glare at his partner.

"What? What is it?" Jacobs gasped, lurching backward.

"We're in trouble. Sure 'nough, the deer is there."

"Okay," Jacobs said, his eyes bulging with anxiety. "But why's that trouble?"

"A scavenger's standin' over it."

"A wha'?" Jacobs sputtered. His expression transformed from concern to pure terror. "What's it doin' this far north?"

"Not sure. But if there's one flesh-eater here, there are more nearby," Titus said, his eyes darting.

"And they're lookin' for us?" Jacobs stuttered, sheer panic on his face.

"Maybe they just want the deer. Let's back up real slow-like and get the hell out of here. We'll head to the rendezvous point and warn the others."

"Right behind ya. But what about Roberts?" Jacobs asked as he shuffled behind Titus.

"Maybe he's seen the scavenger too. I sent him to the other side of the clearing in case we missed the deer. If he's where he should be, he'll see that flesh-eater and head back to the rendezvous, too. Stay close."

"Don't worry 'bout that," Jacobs replied with an audible gulp.

They crept away, doing their best not to make a sound. After no more than fifteen paces, a thunderous crashing of branches and foliage erupted behind them. As they spun around, several forms burst out of the brush.

"RUN!" Titus roared.

They didn't hesitate. Fear drove them forward, crashing down the path, heedless of the noise they made. Their hearts pounded, lungs burned. They knew even a scratch from one of the man-eaters could mean infection. They'd heard the horrific stories all their lives. The thought alone laced their nerves with stomach-churning dread.

Glancing back, Jacobs counted four scavengers. "I see four!" he screamed.

"Means others are ahead or along our flanks. Don't slow down!" Titus yelled.

"You just keep runnin'! I'll keep up!"

Two scavengers burst onto the path twenty yards ahead. Without slowing, Titus veered right into the brush, Jacobs close behind. They clawed through dense underbrush. Thorns tore at their skin and ripped their clothing, but fear dulled the pain.

"We're not gonna make the rendezvous. I'm headin' to lookout number three!" Titus shrieked. Blood trickled from a cut on his hairline, flowing into his eyes. He wiped it away as they ran. A chorus of hideous screeches echoed through the forest.

Usually unshakable, Titus had once downed a charging brown bear with a single arrow. But this shriek made his heart skip a beat. He stumbled, then recovered. "THEY HAVE OUR SCENT!"

"We're screwed. My God, we're totally screwed!" Jacobs cried.

"Cain't be more'n fifty yards from the lookout. We can make it!"

They burst onto a path. Titus turned left and dashed toward a trail intersection. "There it is, come on!"

Throwing his bow over his shoulder, Titus sprinted to a massive Ponderosa pine. Behind it, a rope usually lowered the ladder to the lookout pod above—but it was missing. The ladder dangled freely.

"Get goin'!" Titus barked.

Jacobs scrambled up as Titus helped from below. As he put his foot on the first rung, Titus glanced back. At least eight scavengers appeared at the intersection of the trail.

Paul Jenkins, a resident of Boulderside and fellow hunter, jerked upright in his blind. "Holy mother of God, did ya hear that?"

"Yeah, a scavenger locked onto a blood scent," replied Lawrence Tate, the colony's leader. Boulderside, one of the last surviving North American settlements west of the Mississippi, sat nestled in the Rockies.

Tate, fifty-two, was tall and muscular, with a military bearing and salt-and-pepper hair. He led with calm authority and unflinching courage, never wavering under pressure. But even he felt a chill. Scavengers terrified everyone.

The Rocky Mountain colony had been free from infection for twenty years. Yet the scavenger's cry proved the plague still lived.

"Scavengers? Cain't be. They don't come this far north. They cain't handle the cold," Jenkins pleaded, binoculars raised.

"Not until now," Tate said. "We need everyone back at the rendezvous point."

The colony had moved north to escape the flesh-eaters, who couldn't survive harsh climates. But survival came at a cost. The cold was brutal for the colonists, too.

Jenkins jumped from platform one, descended the ladder, and sent three men down different trails.

Moments later, Tate joined him on the ground. He secured the ladder's retrieval rope and looked up the trail.

Chapter 2

"They're climbin'? They cain't climb," Lawrence Jacobs wailed as he continued up the ladder.

"Hurry man! Get that damn pod door open," bellowed Titus from below.

"I'm tryin', but the stupid thin's stuck," Jacobs screamed in reply. Sweat poured down his face, and the foul odor of fear drenched his body.

Though most of the scavengers mulled around the tree some thirty feet below, bouncing and weaving like a bunch of rowdy drunks looking for a fight, one creature had climbed several rungs. It was jittery and somewhat inept, but he made headway. As soon as there was room on the ladder, another creature followed.

To the Boulderside hunters this was inconceivable. Not because their pursuers were physically incapable, but because their brains weren't supposed to understand the theory of ascending a ladder. The viral infection that plagued them had supposedly stripped away such functions.

Though the colonists possessed a few guns, ammo remained scarce. Gunpowder and shell casings were hard to make and dangerous to store. So, unless their home came under attack, they only used bows, spears, machetes, and knives to hunt.

Titus retrieved an arrow from his quiver, nocked it, and took aim at their pursuer below. He pulled back on the bow's animal-gut stringing and released. SNAP! The weapon twanged with a potent torqued vibration and shot the deadly projectile into the flesh eater's forehead with a thwump. The creature tumbling off the ladder and fell to the ground. The other scavengers took no notice with the next beast quickly taking his place.

Titus threaded another arrow and was getting ready for his next shot when he noticed that the attacker below him had made a conscious decision to change its assault direction. "Did ya see that?" Titus exclaimed.

"No, 'cause I'm too scared to look and I'm tryin' to get in this damn door," Jacobs pleaded as he banged on the entry's latch.

"After I shot the first one, the next one changed its approach. Now he's a'comin up the back of the tree, and I no longer have a shot. That's not s'posed to happen."

Historical references explained that the dim-witted creatures attacked with no thought for their own mortality or to the mortality any of their comrades. Every story or documentation made that clear. Once they found prey, they just attacked head-on without strategizing their pursuit. Now, a scavenger had made an evasive maneuver and Titus's shooting angle had vanished. His bow was no longer a feasible weapon. He placed the arrow back into the quiver and pulled a razor-sharp machete from a sheath at his waist.

Most of the tree's limbs had been cut off to make it difficult, if not impossible, to scale the tree without the ladder. But a couple of thick branches remained on the right and left of the hatch as a staging point for entering and leaving the pod. Titus swung over and climbed on the closest limb to get into a defensible position.

<hr>

"FRED! Oh, my Christ!"

"WHAT? WHAT?" Jacobs screamed. He craned his neck and looked past Titus. Two scavengers were just feet from the men's perch. "Damn it, Titus, I know. They're climbin', and they're close. I'm a'doin' all I can to get this door open."

"No, look at that one on the ground. Look what he's a'doin'," Titus said with an increased alarm.

Jacobs stared in disbelief. One of the creatures on the ground was directing the others—gesturing, snarling, even reacting to being watched.

"That cain't be," Jacobs choked in a small gasp.

"The door! Get that door open, for God's sake!" Titus yelled.

"It won't budge. I think it's locked from the inside," Jacobs answered. His voice cracked with the strain of the situation. He was trembling and drenched with sweat. Urine had stained his pants as fear had sliced control from his bladder.

"Roberts. It's Roberts. God damn it!" Titus snarled. He shoved Jacobs aside and pounded the steel door with the hilt of his machete. CLANG! CLANG! "ROBERTS! OPEN THE DAMN DOOR!"

"I, I cain't do it," came a muffled voice from inside. "The scavengers will get me if'n' I do."

Before Titus could screech the next protest building in his throat, a hand grabbed his shoe. Without thinking, he swung his machete in a downward arc and chopped the attacker's arm clean off at the elbow. The beast didn't scream in pain as any normal person might—they rarely did. It merely reached up with the other hand in its mindless desire to feed. Titus wasted no time and sliced this appendage off as well. He placed his boot on the snarling attacker's head and shoved him off the ladder.

"ROBERTS! Open the door NOW, or ya won't hafta worry 'bout the scavengers because I will frickin' *KILL YA MY SELF!*" Titus yelled.

First came the sound of the latch unhooking, and then the door swung inward. Roberts' terrified face appeared in the opening. "Hurry, hurry, come on, get yar asses in here! Jesus, hurry!" Roberts shrieked as he furiously waved his hand.

"Jenkins, go!" Titus yelled as he turned to face the next ascending scavenger. This one didn't grab at him; this flesh-eater merely sought to chomp down on his leg. Titus chopped down and struck the beast across its neck, almost cleaving the head from its shoulders. The body jerked a few times before falling harmlessly to the ground. Wiping the blade on his pants to prevent blood from splattering into his face, he turned to see Jenkins disappear into the pod.

Titus made one last look below. The next scavenger was still several feet away and he knew he could get to safety before the fiend would reach him. He sheathed his machete and headed up.

Unknown to the sharpshooter, another scavenger had made it three-quarters up and then shifted its direction. Half using the side of the ladder and the stubby wounds of missing tree limbs, the attacker approached the colonist unseen. Just as Titus started to pull his leg into the pod, the hidden assailant sank its teeth into his calf. Titus let out a scream that shook the forest.

———————

Chapter 3

Paul Jenkins scampered back to Larry Tate. Tate, Jeff Peters, Barry Ward, along with brothers Fred and Jerry Dinkins, found a location some thirty yards from where the scavengers were attacking their friends. "Four are lumberin' around the base of the tree. There are also a few bodies on the ground. They look dead," Jenkins said as he recounted his reconnaissance. "There are two more on the tree, maybe three."

Tate nodded in understanding. He then looked over at Peters and Ward; two seasoned colony hunters situated to his right. Tate pointed to the scavenger's right flank. "Get to that stand of shrubs," he said as he pointed to a small patch of vegetation. After receiving their acknowledgment, Tate turned to the Dinkins' brothers. He directed them toward the scavenger's left. "There's a boulder there. Get behind that. I will give each of ya forty-five seconds to get into position. After that, I will give the signal to attack. Be ready and be careful. They all nodded.

The colony leader examined the events around the tree one more time before signaling the side teams to begin their flanking moves. As soon as those groups headed out, he started the countdown. With weapons at the ready, he and Jenkins positioned themselves some fifteen yards away from the frenzied beasts.

"NOW!" Tate yelled as he reached zero in his countdown.

When they heard Tate's bellowing command, most of the scavengers—confused and unsure of what was happening—froze. Their leader, however, didn't hesitate. He scampered past the tree and disappeared into the bushes just as the flanking teams sprung on their unsuspecting prey.

Ward, with machete raised, swung with a heavy blow and cleaved the closest scavenger's head clean off at the shoulders. The body momentarily ran several steps with arms frantically reaching out to find some purchase before falling into a heap and spasming on the ground.

The Dinkins' brothers did a tag-team on another scourge, with Barry shoving a spear straight through the thing's neck and Jerry splitting its grotesque orb in two. Tate and Jenkins used huge claw hammers and quickly dispatched the last two creatures with massive strikes to their skulls.

The scavengers still on the tree looked down and then back up toward the secured door. They seemed unsure what to do. Finally, the lowest one on the tree tried to climb down, but this proved more difficult for the creature than ascending the tree. He lost his grip and fell flat on his back on the ground. Barry Dinkins was there and rammed his spear into its left eye and through the skull. The body jerked a few times, then stopped moving.

The last two scavengers still clinging to the tree began loudly grunting and growling. They started jerking up and down on the ladder as it didn't appear that they could decide what to do without their leader. The lowest of the two finally let go and jumped. He was only about fifteen feet up, but there was a loud snap as his left ankle broke when he hit the ground. Jenkins used his hammer and ended its life with a crushing blow to the side of its skull.

Just then, the last scavenger hit the ground landing right next to Jenkins. Though the colonist immediately spun around to face a possible attack, it became clear that the thing was already dead with an arrow sticking out of the top of his head. Titus had heard the commotion below and opened the hatch for a look. A quick bow shot had ended the confrontation.

The three colonists made their way down the ladder from the pod. Once on the ground Tate sensed something wasn't right. The expressions on the men's faces were a mixture of relief and dire apprehension.

"Did you see the way them scavengers moved?" Jacobs said as he walked up. "And one of them was directing the others up the tree. Did ya see? That cain't be, can it?"

"We'll get to that. There's somethin' else? What's happened?" Tate asked the three.

Jacobs and Roberts now bore similar expressions of resignation. Neither could look Titus in the eyes.

"I asked a question. What's happened?"

"It . . ." Titus started to say before his throat constricted in fear. He swallowed hard and tried again. "It bit me."

"Oh, my dear Christ," Jenkins said as he made the sign of the cross.

"Where? Let me see," Tate said.

Titus turned his leg to reveal a mouth-sized gouge. A scavenger had chomped down and ripped a chunk of flesh from his calf. The wound already showed signs of decay, which meant any chance of amputation to halt the spread had passed. A green pus-like fluid bubbled in and around the damaged flesh, and a spiderweb network of green had begun to race up his veins. Tate looked at Titus. The man had an expression of utter loss.

"Jenkins, take the men and git back to the settlement. Fred, leave your spear," Tate said without further explanation.

There was no argument. The entire group understood what must be done.

After the rest of the team had left, Tate and Titus sat on a couple of large rocks. Neither said a word for several minutes as the reality of what was about to happen sank into both men.

Tate, the executioner.

Titus, the victim.

The extermination had to take place for only one reason. Titus would soon turn into a scavenger and lose all knowledge of his former self and his fellow colonists. All they would be to him was food.

"Larry, I don't blame ya for what ya gotta do," Titus muttered. "There's no other choice. We both know that. But–" his voice cracked as the emotion of the situation flooded him. "Oh god, I don't wanna to die." Joe Titus broke into sobs.

"Christ, Joe. I know that. If'n' there was any other way. Hell, I'd even help ya escape. As far as I'm concerned, ya could become one of those thin's and live whatever life ya could live. But, well, I gotta think about the rest of the colony. I mean, what would ya do in my place?"

Titus slowly lifted his head and, through stifled crying, said, "At least wait 'til I start a'goin' through the change. I hear that ya don't feel nothin' when that happens."

"Okay, Joe," Larry Tate said solemnly.

After sitting in silence for a good ten minutes, Tate could take it no longer. "Joe—do ya need me to do anythin' when I get back? Say anythin' to anyone?"

Titus didn't answer. His head was hung low in obvious despair, but his crying had stopped. Slowly and without warning, the bowman toppled to the ground and rolled onto his back. Tate jumped to his feet and moved close to his friend's side. Titus's body went rigid, stretching to its full length. The prone man's crystal blue eyes, which, seconds before were only filled with tears, were now bulging, and covered with a greenish milky film. Tate stared in horror as Titus's eyes slowly rolled back in his head and then closed.

"Dear God. It's happening already," Tate uttered. Tears flowed down his cheeks, and he began sobbing. He suddenly remembered the spear in his hands. He looked at the weapon in revulsion, and his stomach, which was already knotted, now lurched as the thought of ramming the spike through Titus' skull made him want to vomit. But it was the only sure way to kill the diseased man.

Abruptly, Titus' eyes bolted open, and his lips drew back in a snarl. He grabbed Tate's leg and his mouth opened.

"Forgive me!" Tate sobbed and then thrust his spear directly through the middle of Titus' forehead.

****

———

After ripping his leg away from Titus' death grip, Lawrence Tate collapsed to his knees. Joe was admired and respected back at the colony. This would be a significant loss for everyone, but Larry would feel his absence most of all. He and Titus had been close friends for years. Their bond, which had resulted after a bloody fistfight when they were young teens, was one of the strongest in all the colony. They often knew what the other was going to say before they said it. They were that close and had been friends that long.

Tate leaned forward and threw up. His gut wrenched, and his eyes watered. Three massive convulsions ensued, one after the other, and then it stopped. The big man spit, wiped his mouth, and then stood. He pulled out a small shovel from his backpack and went about burying his friend.

Chapter 4

"Tate's back," Fred Jacobs announced to the community elders gathered in the governing cavern. "He will tell us what to do."

Perry Smith, frail with whisper-thin gray hair and a hooked beak of a nose, jumped to his feet. "We must move! That's what we must do. We canna' take a chance of being infected by these god-forsaken creatures!"

"Now, let's not go off half-cocked with panic," Elder Terry Peters said. "We cain't just pick up and leave every time there's a crisis. And besides, the scavengers cain't maneuver up the slopes to our home. They are incapable of scalin' the steepness of our entry points. Ya know that." Peters, the voice of calm and the colony's previous leader, was Tate's biggest ally in the management and governing of the colony.

Old for the times at seventy-five, Peters still looked the part. Silver-haired with matching beard, both trimmed neatly. Focused brown eyes, which sat behind a pair of square rimmed wire glasses, conveyed wisdom and knowledge. He was a stoic figure who never questioned Tate's directives. In fact, it was Peters that had mentored the current colony leader. When he had hit the mandatory age to vacate his authority, he pushed for Tate as his replacement. And though his backing of the young and brash man rattled many elders, Peters persevered, and Tate became the new person in charge.

"Ya haven't seen what I saw today," Jacobs said with a tremble in his voice. "They climbed number three–straight up."

There were gasps throughout the meeting chamber. Frank Potter, the lead opposition to Tate, rose to his feet and shuffled his rail thin legs to the center of the room. The voices and muttering simmered, and all eyes shifted to the barrel-chested figure. He cleared his voice. "I agree with Terry. Movin' the settlement would be almost impossible. Many of our people are too old, and others simply wouldn't go. No, we must find a way to better hide and secure our entry points. After that, we need to devise a plan for a stronger defense."

Terry Peters threw a sideways glance at the speaker. His mouth sagged open, and his brow furrowed so deep he looked like a human pug. Potter was always the first to go against Tate, and Tate would most assuredly not recommend moving. Peters knew this and sensed something wrong.

"In fact," Potter went on, "Donny Thompson and I been studyin' our defensive strategy for some time and have come up with a better, more effective way of dealin' wit' our resources. Our plan is foolproof and will guarantee victory should anyone or anythin' attack us. I can also promise everyone in this room of no loss of life on our colony's side. So, if'n the elders would give me the authority to change the defensive schemes, I would be glad to take this responsibility from Mr. Tate."

It was at that moment that Terry Peter's confusion screeched to a stop– for there it was. Potter's motive served on a silver platter. Another step in the blustering buffoon's strategy to take control. And though this was clear to him, there were shouts of approval from around the chamber with several faces full of eager hopefulness. Some endorsements came from those already in Potter's circle of influence, but others seemed to climb onboard merely out of fear of what had happened that day. Those who said nothing looked toward Peters for his input. The older man eyed the room's doorway in hopeful anticipation of Tate's arrival, but Tate didn't appear. Shaking his head in resignation, he took a deep breath and stood.

"Listen to me, everyone. It would be unwise to make any decisions until we hear firsthand from Larry what went on. After all, he witnessed the event. And trust me, if'n he believes that Potter's defensive ideas are valid, he will gladly implement them. So, let's stay calm and wait for Larry's return. Which, I might add, will be at any moment," Peters said in a reassuring voice. Once again, Peters expectantly turned his head toward the room's entry.

Chapter 5

January 47, MARS/159

The Mars Settlement City of New Plymouth

Flynn T. Everett stared through a small porthole in the McCain Observatory in New Plymouth, Mars. Named after Paul Thomas McCain, the first science officer to arrive on the planet, the building was a favorite place for Everett. He would often come here to contemplate and decompress. Today, his reasons involved multilayered self-examination.

As he gazed through the glass aperture into the blackness of space, his thoughts should have been consumed with the honor of being named captain of the upcoming trip to Earth. In fact, the thrill of the mission was indeed causing his heart to race and his stomach to flutter in excitement. Yet, other thoughts wrestled their way into his mind, making the elation seem as vacuous as the oxygen-deprived void he stared into.

Though a descendant of the 'Earth-born Originals' landing party of 453, Everett felt more Martian than Earthling. So, the thought of leaving his family and friends, even for the honor of captaining the first starship to return to Earth, provoked an uncontrollable pang of anxiety.

A voyage back to the original home planet had weighed heavily on the minds of many since the colonists landed on the red planet some 159/Mars years earlier. Although these pioneers never expected to go back to Earth—the pipeline was always meant to be a one-way feed for them—none expected that communications from their home would cease altogether. And yet, interaction from the blue planet had discontinued just before the end of their fifth year on Mars. No warning came to prepare the Martians for this event, and the sudden silence caused a somberness many carried throughout their lives.

"We leave in three days. Are all of your affairs in order?" a man's voice said from the doorway of the observatory.

Without turning back to see who spoke, Everett responded, "For the most part, yes." He said nothing more for several seconds before adding, "You know, we do not know what to expect when we land on Earth. I mean, things weren't so good when the Originals left, and things might be much worse now. And have you ever considered why we stopped receiving messages from them? The whole situation gives me pause."

The man at the door said nothing; he didn't need to. They'd had the same conversation many times over the last few weeks.

"I know what you're thinking, but this is our home, our true home, and it's difficult to leave–everything," Flynn confessed.

"Everything? Or a certain someone?" Brad Cummings, Everett's childhood friend and ship's pilot, said.

"Not fair," Flynn said as he turned to face Cummings.

"Flynn, the selection for science officer came about like all the other positions on the vessel. You can't blame the council for not selecting Melanie."

"I can, and I will—to the last moment before we lift off. I will blame each of one of those nearsighted politicians for not putting her on the roster," Flynn said defiantly. "And you're wrong; my name wasn't pulled out of a rabbit's hat like all the rest."

"Really? Are you going to go there? Listen, Flynn, you know as well as I do that Captain Powell's injury left you as the only viable option to helm the M-453/E Star Ship. I mean, if not you, then who?"

Flynn remained outwardly unconvinced and internally boiling mad. The Mars High Council's choice not to give Melanie Canfield the science officer position for the mission was asinine. She was the most qualified, the most seasoned, and, to get to the actual point of his furor, they were soon to be engaged. How could he possibly leave her now? Hadn't he considered every detail for his proposal, right down to the music that would be playing, the right meal to be served, and the words he would use during the big question? At least, that had been the plan before the governing body denied her appointment.

Now, he felt it would be unfair to Melanie to go through with the proposal. Sure, she would probably still say yes, but he didn't believe it was the right thing to do. What if he didn't return? The whole situation ate at him. Every time he thought he knew the answer, he'd change his mind.

Flynn ignored Brad's retort about his appointment as captain and strode to the extensive electronic mapping table in the center of the room. He stood rigid and unrelenting as he positioned himself in front of the unit.

Tapping an icon on the control console he said, "Milky Way Galaxy Map–on." Instantly, a 3D diagram of the solar system map materialized and floated above the table. Flynn began waving both hands in the air like the conductor of a 40-piece orchestra. He moved his arms in various directions, reaching up and down and back and forth until the galaxy had dissected to reveal their solar system as the central focal point of the map. Pulling back the sleeve of his shirt, he tapped several sensors on the face of his watch-sized interface wrist unit and then glanced back to the map. After a few seconds, a dashed route line from Mars to the Earth appeared.

"Brad?" Flynn said, the anger having mostly ebbed from his voice.

"Yes?"

"I've been thinking. If we start here," Flynn said, indicating a position on the floating map, then pointed to a place several hundred kilometers beyond the red planet's surface. "With Mars in this position. See?"

"Yes," Brad said, somewhat vaguely. He walked closer to the hovering schematic.

"If we reach maximum speed and then use our planet's gravitational pull to slingshot around the planet," Flynn said, "the action will give us a twenty-seven percent increased velocity. Once we leave our gravity field on the other side, the additional speed will cut our travel time to Earth significantly, not to mention considerable fuel savings."

Brad studied the map for a moment and watched as Flynn hit several more sensors. When he finished, a second route became visible. The flight plan's original course was highlighted yellow and set up as dashes. Everett's alternative path displayed as green dots. The two routes made illuminated runs with the green track rapidly surpassing the yellow course once it left Mars' orbit.

"Indeed," Brad said, as he studied the diagram carefully. "That should work—well done, Flynn. The new trajectory should allow us to arrive at Earth fifteen to twenty days sooner. I'll present the route to the planning committee for a thorough review and testing."

"Sounds great," Flynn replied. "And while you're at it, make sure my choice for science officer is added to the mission roster."

Brad started to respond to Everett's latest frivolous attempt to goad but ignored the remark. "Later," he said, and left the room.

Flynn studied the map a while longer before tapping it off. He returned to the portal and gazed toward Earth one last time. As he stared into the darkness, he caught his reflection in the glass and frowned. Saying goodbye to Melanie was going to be the most challenging thing he'd ever done.

On his way out, Flynn grabbed his Electro-Infapad and said, "On." The voice activation system recognized his speech, and the pad lit up. He waited a moment as data populated and then said, "Open G-force parameter and Earth new flight simulation updates." The Infapad began displaying information. Flynn studied the notes he had previously added to the simulation. Head down as he scanned the pad, he left the observatory and moved toward the launch command center. He passed through the double doors leading to the walkway between the two buildings, just as Melanie Canfield walked in.

Flynn almost passed her without noticing when he heard her utter a simple, "Ahem."

"Mel!" Flynn said as he pulled up abruptly. "I didn't see you."

"No kidding." Sarcasm clear in her words.

"I'm sorry." He leaned over for a quick kiss. "Where you headed?"

"On my way to find you."

"How d'you know I'd be here?"

"I bumped into Brad as he headed toward the command center. He said you were here."

"Yeah, he and I were discussing an alternative flight strategy. He's going to present it to the flight planners for review."

"He told me. Said you've sliced quite a few days away." Melanie offered an encouraging smile.

"Maybe. If the simulations prove accurate," Everett said matter-of-factly.

"I'm sure they'll verify your findings. Listen, I came looking for you to tell you I ran into Sanchez in the commissary," she said, her words iced with disdain.

"Yeah, what did Gary-the-grump have to say today? That he got screwed out of going on the mission–again?"

"Sort of. Only this time, our friend tried a new tactic. He used the council's snub toward me as a springboard into how we both got the shaft. He subtly suggested that *we* should go together to file a complaint."

Flynn's left eyebrow rose. "What did you say?"

"I told him it wouldn't do any good. We all agreed that the selection process for all the qualified individuals would be a lottery. We have no grounds for filing a grievance."

"If it were anyone but him, I'd say it'd be worth a try. But the troll has no business going on the flight. He came close to failing some of the most fundamental tests during training. Besides, he's a damn jerk," Flynn spouted through clenched teeth, causing a face muscle to bulge. "Just thinking about that guy irritates me to no end. Did I mention that he's a jerk?"

"A damn jerk is what I think you said. Anyway, I wanted to come and tell you about our conversation because I don't think the council, or you for that matter, have heard the last from him. He's bound to cause more trouble. You have time for coffee?"

"I'll make time," Flynn said with a smile. He then bent down and kissed her again, this time with passion.

"Yummy," Melanie cooed as Flynn pulled back. Her face flushed, and her eyes sparkled. "When we're alone, later, I fully expect to receive much more of that."

Flynn grinned, and the two walked from the observatory to the commissary. They got two coffees, stepped onto the patio, and sat down at a table positioned just above a walkway encircling the campus' small park.

The almost one-acre parcel provided an Earth-like setting. Artificial grass, green and plush, had an authentic feel. A well-maintained flower garden sat in the center with a small bubbling water fountain. A jogging trail ran along the park's perimeter. Strategically located around the path, some thirty feet away on average, rose four large complexes. These buildings housed the science and biosphere monitoring facilities, the aerospace command center, and the observatory.

An eight-inch-thick high-density glass and Veeron shield covered the entire complex. Martian scientists used resources on Mars to develop Veeron—a coating like Teflon from Earth, but much harder and not susceptible to breaking down due to excessive heat. This defensive layer was the original piece of what became a two-part atmospheric protection system for the Mars settlement. The first shield was sealed and anchored along the outside of the perimeter buildings. This barrier's base sank fifty meters into the oxidized iron dust and rock that made up Mars' surface.

Dome-shaped, the shield rose 100 feet and sheltered all areas traversed on foot by the local populace. Attached to the outer layer of this screen was a thin sheet of photochromic film treated with an ingenious colorization process. This layer changed colors depending on the time of day. During daylight hours, the magnificent coating radiated with a light sky-blue tint, giving the inhabitants the impression of atmosphere and sky like Earth's. As the sun set, the color of the glass gradually changed until it became translucent. The view had the semblance of a clear nighttime sky. All the other settlement communities possessed this same shielding and colorization film for all areas.

Transportation to nearby settlements, those ten kilometers or less, occurred through transport tubes of the same Veeron material. A magnetic rail system ran to and from the populated parts of the planet within those cylinders. The cars running on the rails were self-contained units able to accommodate up to 50 passengers. For travel between settlements on other parts of the planet, the inhabitants used the interplanetary M453 fleet.

A second "skin" or protective shield had been added much later as the Martian technology advanced. This active layer boasted an ultra-high density "energy field." Composed of nucleonic particles, this barrier allowed the inhabitants to maintain an artificial breathable atmosphere over a much larger area. Whereas the solid shield stopped at the rear of the main buildings and the transportation tubes, this new buffer zone often extended over 100 meters or more beyond the furthest outbuilding of the settlement.

The Martian engineer's latest innovation gave the residents additional freedom of space they did not enjoy with the original shields. Both protective barriers were designed so the gravitational system of the settlements operated to their optimum capabilities, allowing inhabitants to maintain a livable oxygen atmosphere. The field could also be expanded through electronic manipulation to accommodate settlement growth.

Flynn and Melanie sat at their table and discussed the mission, avoiding the uncomfortable point that she wasn't on the roster. Just as the two were finishing their coffees, Gary Sanchez and High Council member Michael Walker came out of the command center. As they walked, Sanchez began waving his arms while gesturing toward the sky. Walker seemed to listen intently until suddenly, as if provoked, Sanchez hopped in front of Walker and blocked his path. He began jabbing the shorter, much older man's chest with his finger. Sanchez's face twisted in rage and flushed red.

Flynn and Melanie heard Sanchez shouting with vulgar expletives littering the tirade. At one point, Walker stepped back and put his arm up as if he intended to protect himself from an imminent attack.

"Are you seeing this?" Melanie said in surprise.

"Yep." And with that, Flynn jumped from his chair and leaped over the patio railing some 20 feet to the ground. In one fluid motion, he hit the surface, went into a tuck and roll, and sprung back to his feet and with legs already churning. He raced at break-neck speed toward the pair of combatants.

When Flynn got within a few meters, Walker noticed him. The councilman's eyes went wide in recognition, not only of seeing Flynn coming but of the almost inevitable confrontation. Sanchez caught this reaction and realized someone was bearing down on them. He balled up his fist and spun around expectantly to meet the intruder. This was all Flynn needed to see. The physically superior Everett crashed into Sanchez's chest and tackled him to the ground. As the two slammed onto the artificial grass, Flynn grabbed Sanchez's arm and wrenched it backward. He then rolled the panicked Sanchez over until his face was firmly smashed onto the artificial turf.

With his knee on the groaning man's back, Flynn twisted Sanchez's arm—just enough to get his attention. The move produced the desired effect as the pinned man screamed in pain.

"Everett, stop it," Walker pleaded. "You'll break his arm!"

"I'll do more than that in a minute," Flynn insisted through gritted teeth.

"Flynn," Melanie said firmly as she approached the two. "Let Gary up."

After a few intentional moments of hesitation, Flynn let out a long, if not disgusted, breath. "Gary, I'm going to let you up. If you start anything, I'll toss you back on the ground and break your arm–

and don't think I won't. Are you going to be a good boy, or should I just snap your arm now and get it over with?"

"You bastard, I'm going to kick your—," Sanchez started. But before the next word left his mouth, Flynn yanked on the man's appendage, this time with a bit more emphasis. "OK, OK! Stop, please. I promise; I won't do anything. For God's sake, stop!"

Flynn released Sanchez and, in one fluid movement, popped up from the ground and moved over to Melanie and Walker, no less for the wear.

Sanchez shifted his aching arm, rolled over on his back, and moaned. His face was contorted in pain, with a big red mark running down the side of his temple where it had been planted on the turf.

"I think you've permanently damaged my arm," Sanchez snarled. "I can barely move it."

"You're lucky that's all I did. What the hell is going on here?" Everett snapped.

"What's going on here is **NONE** of your damn business!" Sanchez barked back.

"Anytime I see a member of the High Council being accosted by a raving lunatic, someone who appears ready to do bodily harm, I make it my business," Flynn said as he took a menacing step towards Sanchez.

Walker grabbed Flynn by the arm and held him back. "Mr. Sanchez was simply trying to convince me to persuade the other council members to name him navigator on the mission," Walker said in explanation. "I told him he certainly deserved the position, as did

Adrian Jones, Mary Buford, and Paul Renault. However, the lottery selection went to Paul, and I could do nothing about the outcome."

"You promised me!" Sanchez yelled, still on the ground and holding his left arm. He was writhing back and forth like someone trying to escape from a straitjacket.

"I did no such thing," Walker said evenly. "Think about what you are suggesting. Even if you were correct, I have no authority to make any promises without the council's approval. I am but one of many that make these decisions."

Sanchez finally stopped thrashing about and wobbled to his feet. His arm hung down by his side like a limp rag. The man was typically frumpy, if not scruffy looking by Martian standards, but now he was all that and more. His hair stood up in all directions, his clothes had two mangled rips that exposed scraped skin, and the heel of one of his shoes was missing. The red streak on his face was now accompanied by blotchy patches of pink on his forehead and neck where his anger had riled his blood pressure.

Staring maliciously at each of the three, Sanchez looked as though he was about to let loose a torrent of venomous expletives. However, he simply sneered, said nothing, and abruptly turned and stomped off. He held his arm and limped away in a jerky step-hop-step-hop manner because of the height difference in shoe heels.

After a few steps, he turned his head and growled over his shoulder, "The three of you will pay for this; just wait and see. And if you think you're going on this trip without me, you've got another thing coming!"

Chapter 6

After Sanchez was out of earshot, Melanie deadpanned, "Why did he include me in his threat; I did nothing?"

"Guilt by association, I'm afraid," Flynn said.

"Great," Melanie scoffed.

"I'm sure Mr. Sanchez meant nothing by his actions. He's just upset. If he put this in the right perspective, he would understand that if this operation goes well, and you all return safely…" Walker hesitated before quickly adding, "… like I'm sure you will, other missions will be scheduled. He'll have new chances just like the others not going on this trip."

"Don't worry, Mike, we'll come back," Flynn said with a smile.

"I know you will," Walker replied with as much enthusiasm as he could. The council member put his hand on Everett's shoulder. "Flynn, many of those on the board secretly hoped this mission would be aborted.

"Though most young Martian inhabitants are passionate about going to Earth, the elders were unsure what might be found. With almost 295 Earth years having passed since our last communication, they were concerned that things there might be— 'complicated'. And, considering that the last messages from Earth were rife with dark and ominous forebodings, I can't say that I blame them."

Flynn knew what was coming; he'd heard the stories on more occasions than he cared to count. However, this was Walker, and he respected the man and his concerns.

Walker explained, "After only 100 days since departure, the space travelers received news that the United States was pressed into declaring war on China. American citizens had no desire to get into another worldwide conflict. Unfortunately, the Chinese forced their respective government's hands. The Red Army attack on Germany, a U.S. ally and ironically the last country to attempt global rule, mandated the war edict.

"Over the next few years, battles occurred mainly in Europe, Asia, and Africa, as previous world wars had done. But then the Chinese, whose armed forces totaled over 6 million men, invaded Alaska. After quickly capturing the state, they swept through western Canada, Washington State, Oregon, Northern California, and parts of Nevada. Soon after these incursions, all communication between the Originals and Earth ended.

"These encroachments took place during year five on Mars and in the year 2062 on Earth. No contact has been received since. You must see how this knowledge has caused much debate about going back?" Walker finished.

"Of course. Yet, everyone must also know that one day we'd have to attempt the trip just to know what had happened," Flynn said.

"Yes, and, well, here we are. Is your team ready?"

"Yes sir," Flynn said hesitantly.

"Uh oh, what is it?" Walker asked as he looked the young captain in the eyes.

"Sir, it's the matter of weapons," Flynn said flatly.

"Oh yes, the armaments issue. You want to take more than just the compression laser pistols. Mr. Cummings has been blasting my com-link since the council denied the taking of larger more powerful weapons," Walker said.

"A decision made by people not going on the mission, I might add," Flynn countered.

The three began walking back toward the commissary. With a look of genuine concern and thought, Walker said, "Yes, well, you and Mr. Cummings will be happy to hear that I am bringing the weapons issue up for another vote this afternoon. I'm personally not convinced that being heavily armed is such a good idea. Yet, as you say, I am not the one traveling 40 million miles from home."

"I couldn't have stated my case any better," Flynn said, a small yet anguished smile forming.

"Don't get too excited; I can't guarantee the additional weapons will be approved. By the way, Mr. Everett…"

Walker rarely called him Mr. Everett unless he was about to bring up a difficult situation or to lecture him.

"Do you know why very few weapons exist on Mars today?"

Flynn did, but again let Walker have his moment. "It's because the Originals destroyed the ones they possessed. They believed if no one owned a shooting weapon, no shooting deaths could occur. They thought the decision to be a straightforward solution to a real and dangerous issue. One they could implement while they were still a small colony.

"After they confirmed no threatening life forms inhabited Mars, they destroyed all the guns in their arsenal. Fast-forward almost 300 years, and we've had almost no fatalities caused by another human being, and of course none with a gun. With a population of nearly 250,000 people, that's saying a lot," Walker finished.

"Yet we do not know what we might encounter once we arrive on Earth. Mike, protection for my crew is my paramount concern here. If we will not have access to all tools necessary to protect ourselves when we visit other worlds, then why have them at all? It seems illogical to me," Flynn responded.

"And that is the very reason the few weapons you will take were designed and built. We wanted you to have at least some protection. But you must know that even getting those was a struggle. It went against over 250 years of history and convention. The decision was a major shift away from our societal philosophies."

After a few more steps, Walker sighed slightly, and then added, "We shall see what the rest of the council has to say about it. Now, I must leave you."

The three said their goodbyes and Walker headed toward the Meeting Center leaving Melanie and Flynn to contemplate the mission, the weapons, and their encounter with Gary-the-grump on their own.

"So, what was that whole flying 'He-Man' attack thing?" Melanie teased as they watched Walker go.

"Seemed like taking that jerk down was the right thing to do at the time," Flynn offered, a tinge of embarrassment in his tone.

"Well, if anyone needed an ass-whipping, he did. But what if he retaliates? He's brilliant and intellectual in some areas, not so much in others. He has that "fine-line" kind of personality. Could jump off the deep end and cause problems at any time," Melanie said with genuine concern.

"Are you saying he lacks common sense?" Flynn interjected.

"He makes me nervous, and he's a bit off. That's all I'm saying. Especially when it comes to this trip. There's no telling what he might try. I wouldn't put it past him to make a bunch of noise to have you removed from the mission because of your attack on him."

"I don't think he possesses the guts," Flynn said with a scoff. After a moment of reflection, he added, "But...to be on the safe side, we'll report the incident. It's better to have it on record from us before he puts his spin on the event."

The two grabbed hands and made their way to the closest transference tube. Once at the station, they signaled a hovering transference drone and requested a transport unit for a ride home. A few minutes passed and then an alert sounded, announcing a tram. A low hum began, and the vehicle came into view. Just as the car came to a stop, Melanie's com-link beeped.

Melanie looked at Flynn and frowned. "Should I answer?"

"Your call," Flynn replied, although he feared it would probably mean another late dinner.

Melanie shrugged her shoulders and tapped the small tab on her jacket's lapel, "Lieutenant Commander Canfield."

"Ms. Canfield, it's Gene Hemming," a voice said.

"Yes, sir. What can I do for you?" Her stomach felt on the verge of twisting. Had they heard about Flynn's encounter with

Sanchez already? Flynn tilted his head in wonder as he regarded Melanie.

"Are you with Captain Everett, by chance?"

"Yes sir, we're together at Transport Station number five."

"The governing board needs you and Captain Everett to come to the Council Meeting Center right away. Is that possible?" The urgency was clear in Hemming's voice.

"Yes, of course. Is something wrong?" Melanie asked. She looked at Flynn and mouthed, Uh-Oh.

"The council will explain upon your arrival. We'll be expecting you."

Her com-link went silent.

"Boy, are you in trouble," Flynn said.

"Shut up," Melanie grumbled as she punched Flynn playfully on the shoulder. "They want you too, don't forget. I'm guessing your wrestling buddy Gary Sanchez filed a complaint against you and you're about to get a verbal thrashing."

"I don't think so. Too soon. Besides, it was your com-link they signaled."

"Whatever," Melanie said in mock surrender.

The two left the station and walked toward the Meeting Center. Even after many visits, the building still impressed. The twelve-foot-tall entry doors of Martian polymer compositions resembled oak wood from Earth. Their size was an intimidating greeting that precluded the many important decisions that had been made inside.

The octagonal-shaped entry area had a floor made of Martian marble. Polished to a mirror-like finish. The natural stone contained red veins running through a bright white background. The walls were twenty meters high and lined with pictures of the many generations of Earth and Martian pioneers, as well as past and current elder leaders. The significance of these portraits could not be denied and left many in profound admiration.

Across the room stood another entryway. These slightly less expansive doors led into the main conference chamber. Positioned above this entry hung a dynamic pose of Captain Gerard Hurley. Hurley had been the captain of the PIONEER-1 spaceship that the Originals arrived in. Known as Mars' version of Christopher Columbus, his name appeared on plaques and monuments throughout the many Mars settlements. Flynn always felt a moment of admiration and respect when he entered this building and saw this picture, especially since being named captain of the return expedition.

Flynn and Melanie crossed the empty area before stopping at the doors below the image. Both doors contained one-foot square windows. They glanced at each other, nodded, and picked a window to peer through. A stern-faced Walker stood at the podium before a full chamber. Their friend and benefactor appeared to be caught up in an animated presentation. To Walker's right, a man jumped to his feet and pointed an accusatory finger in Walker's direction.

"Holy crap!" Flynn whispered.

"What is it?" Melanie asked, her brow furrowing as she scanned the hall.

"It's Sanchez's uncle, Paulo. I'll bet they're arguing about his nephew. I'm sure he's demanding an explanation why Gary didn't get selected to go on the mission."

"And they need us for that?" Melanie derided.

"Not likely. But I'm pretty confident that's what's happening now."

Just then, the door opened toward Flynn. He and Melanie jumped back and out of the way. An attendant, who stood off to one side of the inner chamber, had noticed the two and opened the doors exposing the 'Peeping Toms'. All heads turned and stared at Everett and Canfield. They were like trapped rats with no escape.

Alfred Barnes, the Sitting Chairperson of the Council, waved them forward. "Captain Flynn, Lieutenant Canfield, please come in and make your way to the podium next to Councilman Walker." The statesman's demanding baritone voice caused the invitees to rush forward like people accused of some dastardly deed.

"Yes sir, but what's this all about?" Flynn asked as he hurried to Walker's side.

Barnes raised a hand. "Patience, Captain Flynn, things will be explained soon." He turned his attention back to the still-agitated Sanchez. "Mr. Sanchez, you've passionately stated your case for your nephew with great care and thought, and the council will take your presentation into account. But now, two additional issues must be discussed without further delay," Barnes said as he moved to end the man's fervent plea.

Sanchez tried to object, but Barnes spoke over his challenge, "First things first. Lieutenant Commander Canfield, please step forward."

Melanie took a stiff step up and turned toward Barnes. The man grimaced slightly and said, "A difficult decision needed to be made, and it concerns you."

"Me?" Melanie asked in confusion as she glanced back at Flynn.

"It has come to our attention that the science officer designated for the voyage to Earth, Second Lieutenant Francine Templeton, is pregnant. Therefore, we must replace the crewman for the upcoming mission. Ms. Canfield, you have trained alongside the second lieutenant since the trip was announced, hence the council believes you should be her replacement. That is if you still desire to go." Barnes tried to keep a concerned expression but couldn't stop the corners of his lips from turning up slightly.

Stunned by this announcement, Melanie could barely speak. At first, all she could muster was a drawn-out, "Uh. . . uh. . ."

"Melanie," Flynn prodded.

"I'm sorry, of course. It would honor me to accept the decision by the High Council," she finally blurted, wiping a long strand of hair away from her face.

Paulo Sanchez made a chuffing noise in apparent unreserved disdain.

"The entire governing membership thanks you," Barnes offered as he ignored the glowering Sanchez. "You are to report to the shuttle at 06:00 tomorrow morning. You may sit."

"Yes sir, I'll be there," Melanie said as she dashed to an empty chair next to the podium.

"Now, Captain Everett," Barnes started, his voice had a clear somberness to it. "Councilman Walker has pleaded your case regarding additional weapons on the mission. As you are fully aware, this request concerns us greatly."

"May I ask why, sir?" Everett said.

"Captain Everett, you are returning to our home planet. After scanning the surface and finding it hospitable, you should be welcomed with open arms. Bringing along an arsenal of weapons might send the wrong message. As you are fully aware, the committee did a thorough investigation of the ship's security, as well as your crew's experience with weapons. We are confident that small munitions are all you will need," Barnes clarified.

Flynn considered this comment beyond ridiculous—they were traveling millions of miles from Mars to what type of environment? They couldn't possibly guess. Not being able to defend his crew if they encountered hostile inhabitants seemed risky and reckless.

Instead of responding with a flippant remark like his younger self would have done, he considered the situation for a moment and then turned to face the 20-member council. His lips creased, and his jaw clenched as he stared into the faces of men who had conceivably never left the confines of Mar's safety enclosures.

After several uncomfortable moments, Flynn finally swiveled back toward Barnes and spoke. "Chairman Barnes and distinguished members of the council. I understand the underlying significance of

———————

the Council's hesitation to arm the mission with additional weapons. However, our planet has not received a single communication from Earth in five-plus generations. We could be entering a hostile environment…"

"Then don't land. Just turn around and come back," one of the council members interjected from the back of the room.

Flynn, in a definitive gesture worthy of a captain, said, "With all due respect, to travel almost forty million miles just to wave at the planet and return home seems unreasonable to me. Does the council want us to just do a fly-by? Do you think the Martian citizens would be satisfied if we returned without the slightest hint of what happened to our species' home planet? Why go at all if we are not committed to finding out the truth," Flynn retorted, his voice commanding but still respectful.

Several conversations broke out around the room. The mingling comments sounded like a buzzing hive of bees that had just been poked with a stick. Walker stared at Flynn, shook his head ever so slightly, and then moved back to the podium to help restore order.

After getting the floor settled, Walker said, "Chairman Barnes, may I?" Barnes nodded in the affirmative. Walker turned and faced the still grumbling group. "I believe Captain Everett makes a valid point. If we are asking these brave men and women to bring us answers, then we cannot ignore the aspects of self-preservation. To that end, I think all of us in this room would agree that the safety of the crew should be foremost in all our plans and preparations. Therefore, I believe a vote for approval of the additional armament should occur now, though I believe the outcome of the vote should be a mere formality."

Chapter 7

Flynn and Melanie rode home filled with giddy jubilation. Getting the okay to bring along the larger cache of weapons had been a win, and in Flynn's mind, needed to happen. However, of equal importance was the declaration of Melanie's appointment as the mission's science officer. But this decision by the Martian Council had one other explosive development, a revival of a previous plan. The engagement!

"I can't stop smiling. This is so unbelievable," Melanie said through an uncontainable grin.

"I know. Honestly, I've been hounding everyone that would listen to get this to happen. The talks often got a little heated. Had I known it would only take getting Betty Canfield pregnant…"

Melanie rolled her eyes and smirked. "You really think you're hot stuff, don't you?"

"I wasn't speaking of me getting her pregnant. Is that what you thought I meant? I am appalled," Flynn said sardonically.

"Yeah, sure you are," Melanie mocked. She began twitching her lips back and forth and then said in contemplation, "I have so much to do. Lots of packing and preparing. Not sure I'm going to get much sleep tonight."

Flynn almost commented on assuring her of that but stopped short. Melanie might think he was just making a typical male remark about them staying up to have sex before the trip and would probably slug him. Yet, having sex that night after his engagement proposal would definitely be in the cards. Flynn slyly grinned but said nothing.

The transport tram stopped at their residential housing area, 4 West, named for its proximity to the rest of the settlement, and the two got off. They strolled over to the community's pantry outlet in the lower level of their housing unit and ordered two flagons of their favorite Martian wine, House of Plymouth Sauvignon.

While there, Melanie canceled her weekly grocery order until further notice. She and Flynn had previously reduced their normal deliveries by half, due to his anticipated upcoming absence. But now, with both going, any new deliveries would have to cease entirely.

With these arrangements made, the two headed to their building's lift station. The complex's dumb-waiter system would deliver the wine. Their droid, Marc Antony, would have placed it in their climate-controlled wine chiller even before they made it to their front door. The robust rose-colored liquid would be pre-cooled to their preferred 17 degrees Celsius and ready to be served once they changed clothes for the evening.

Marc Antony, named after the Roman General from Earth's ancient history, was an M12-B class android. This droid was the closest likeness to a human the Martians possessed. Every physical feature, down to the last hair follicle, resembled a human. However, unlike their human counterparts, whose various shapes, sizes, hair color, and other features set them apart from other human inhabitants, Martian droids were identical looking.

The droids were the same height, shape, had the same facial features, and hair. Their eye color was the same, their feet and hands were proportionately equal, and without clothes, they had the same body features. The droids answered to their name, of course, but they also had a numbered patch on every uniform they owned. That number was also tattooed on their scalp and right shoulder blade.

Those physical identifiers made it simple to tell the droids apart by their human owners. But what made these beings unique from one another was that their personality profiles and functions could be programmed in multiple ways to suit their owners. Engineers could encode the droids to be as interactive as the customer wanted. The ability to perform certain functions their human counterparts wanted them to accomplish could be added as needed.

As Melanie and Flynn rode the lift to their floor, Flynn kissed her neck with small soft touches of his lips. Inching up and down slowly and with purpose, he stopped just below her ear, and then slipped down to the curve of her neck.

"Mmm. . ." Melanie sighed. "That's—"

"Nice?" Flynn interjected.

"Uh-huh, but more like *very* nice."

Flynn continued the gentle kisses across her cheek until he reached her mouth. As she leaned back against the lift's wall, he whisked his lips against hers before softly kissing them. He used his lips to search hers, touching and prodding with light and tender caresses, until Melanie wrapped her arms around his neck and pulled him tight. They kissed passionately until a noise behind them brought them out of their embrace.

"Uh, don't you two live here?" the woman's voice asked.

Flynn turned to see their neighbor, Mrs. Peterson, standing at the opening of the lift. The magnetic elevator had stopped, and the doors had parted with a soft whoosh. These events had gone unnoticed by the two lovebirds. Nor did they notice the slender, silver-haired lady waiting impatiently to get on. Peterson possessed deep wrinkles around her mouth, making it appear that she was perpetually frowning. Her husband of forty years had died the year before, and with or without the wrinkles, she was less than enthused by this display.

"Um, yes, Mrs. Peterson, you know we do," Flynn said, his face flushed.

"You are right Mr. Everett. I *do* know you live here," the woman said in a narrowed tone. "So, I think you should do what you were doing in the privacy of your own home. Yes?"

"Yes ma'am, sorry," Melanie said as she rushed past the woman.

"Young people today, no sense of decency," Mrs. Peterson clucked as she entered the lift.

Once the doors closed and the two were sure the lift had departed, Flynn and Melanie giggled. The light chuckle turned into a hardy laugh, which soon produced laughter-induced tears running down both of their cheeks.

They moved down the hall, both still chuckling as they reached their door. The entryway's sensor scanned them, identified them, and slid the door open. Their interior foyer lights flashed on, then dimmed to a soft glow once they passed through. All sections of the house worked this way. If the occupants were in an area, the lights remained active to their pre-set brightness.

Their apartment was not overtly lavish, but far from modest. The pair had all the conveniences that people of their stature could earn. There was a holographic waterfall scene on the far wall of the main living space that provided a soothing visual and audio experience. This scene could be changed to offer a variety of effects and moods, including a rumbling rain and thundershower that invigorated and awed. Low-backed synthetic seating in the room, similar to Earth's suede, could accommodate up to eight people when entertaining.

Situated in the middle of the room was a round table measuring some four feet across. The table contained electronic interactive components that could be activated with a tap on the owner's wrist interface units. Once initiated, the table unit could provide a dazzling 3 D Sensaround Viewing System. Once triggered, you could watch virtual performers as they moved around the scene.

Though the action was smaller in scale to accommodate the room size, it was as if you were there, live. Scents and temperatures were automatically adjusted and brought the guests deep into the realm of the action.

Flynn and Melanie entered their large living area from the hall, and Marc Antony, who had been alerted by the entry door sensor, appeared.

"Good evening to you both. I trust your day was rewarding," the Android said in a polite and refined voice while bowing.

"Oh, brother, whom are you supposed to be today?" Flynn said with a sigh.

"I should think it to be obvious; Alfred Pennyworth, of course," the droid professed, this time in his routine, relaxed manner, and voice.

"Alfred Pennyworth, who the heck is that M.A.?" Melanie asked.

"Bruce Wayne's butler," the droid answered as if dismayed.

"Somebody's been watching classic Earth movies again," Flynn chuckled as he headed towards the kitchen.

"Oh, Batman's valet. I should have figured as much," Melanie said as she followed him.

"The wine is in the Chiller and your meal of roast duck, lamb shanks, and sweet Thai chili Shrimp is in the warming silo," Marc Antony said, once again using the valet's inflections.

"You know, your sense of humor is getting worse, not better," Flynn insisted as he grabbed two glasses from the glass rack.

"Really, and I thought you would find quite a lot of wit in my fictitious selections for the menu. Aren't they good choices? —I'm not sure I will ever be funny," the droid mused, then turned away dejected.

Flynn and Melanie acquired Marc Antony once they moved in together four years earlier. He had been downloaded with the latest human traits available, including the closest application of the ever-elusive "human-sense-of-humor." This function continued to be a work in progress. Joke telling was not the issue. Droids could deliver a written punch line often better than many humans. The real problem arose as engineers tried to implant that intrinsic human instinct and ability to understand when to use humor and wit in everyday situations and conversations. Marc Antony strove to master this concept.

"Don't worry; most humans aren't all that funny either. You're above the curve, M.A.," Melanie said.

"So, what are we really having because I'm starving," Flynn pleaded.

"Braised cabbage, sauteed onions in wine sauce, and... wait for it...T-Bone steaks."

"Are you still joking or are you now being serious?" Flynn asked skeptically.

"Not joking in the least. Mr. Walker sent the steaks over. They arrived with a note, 'Bon Voyage, my dear friends. Safe trip and look forward to your return."

"Wow, real T-Bone steaks? Must have set him back a pretty Martian Daler or two," Melanie admitted.

Martian Dalers, which was a derivative name of the Dollar currencies that some countries on Earth used, was the planet's only currency. Its origin dated back to 17th century Scandinavia on Earth and was unanimously accepted as a non-conflict term. Dalers kept their original values, never inflating or deflating the entire time on Mars.

With only a small herd of various breeds of livestock, mainly kept for research, meat was more than a luxury and was very expensive. The only time they slaughtered an animal was if it was too old or the stock grew too big. With limited natural resources, it was impossible to keep a large animal populace. And though technology had allowed them to produce artificial meats from other plant proteins, getting a real steak was an extravagance beyond compare.

"I will serve dinner in twenty minutes." Marc Antony said, as he made his way behind the serving bar to the kitchen.

Flynn went to the wine cooler and dispensed the impeccably chilled liquid into the two fluted glasses. He handed one to Melanie, grabbed his glass, and then took her by the hand and led her out to the balcony.

"Hey, what's going on?" Melanie said.

"Whatever do you mean?" Flynn replied coyly.

An ornately decorated table was positioned centrally on the balcony adorned with the couple's best tableware. Two slender soy candles burned softly in the center of the table with their flickering glow giving the entire area a romantic ambiance.

Melanie stared at the spread in amazement. "This was supposed to be a going-away dinner for you or—" But before she finished her sentence, a holographic image of the couple's favorite jazz band suddenly materialized in the corner of the balcony. A strand of party lights appeared around the patio and then a staggered grouping of balloons and streamers.

Melanie cocked her head slightly as she tried to figure out what Flynn was up to. As she turned back for an explanation, the leader of the band nodded to the rest of the group, prompting the drummer to start tapping on his electronic snare drum. After a few beats, the rest of the musicians joined in on a rendition of 'Orion's Paradise.'

Melanie saw Marc Antony peeking through the kitchen window. His smile was as big and broad as a large moon-shaped slice of watermelon.

"Ok, what the hell is going on?" Melanie said as she turned toward Flynn. The man had dropped to one knee and was holding out a small black box with the lid open. I took a moment to for the Melanie's mind to register what Flynn was doing. Then, with her stomach rolling like a gymnast doing multiple front flips, she tilted her head down and gazed at a brilliant 2-carat Martian diamond engagement ring.

"Melanie Ann Canfield, I love you with all my heart. I intend to love you today, tomorrow, forever. I adore you and intend to lavish you with love and affection until my last breath. Will you be my wife?"

Melanie gaped at the sparkling gem as her right hand shot up to the side of her face. For a long moment, she only gawked at the ring, speechless. Finally, she swallowed hard, and breathlessly answered with a resounding, "YES!"

Flynn stood, gently grabbed her left hand, and placed the pre-sized ring on her finger. Pulling her close to him, he kissed her with unrelenting passion.

Marc Antony, having watched the entire scene unfold, came rushing out with his hands in position to clap. Melanie heard the footsteps, shot him a glance, and the droid abruptly spun around on his heels and raced back to the kitchen. Though admonished for the intrusion, the droid pranced and danced as he praised the two's upcoming union.

Chapter 8

"Uncle, this is utter hypocrisy. How could you let them do this to me?" Gary Sanchez bellowed. He paced back-and-forth, snarling like a rampaging silver-backed gorilla. His normally pale skin was once again blotchy red with beads of sweat forming across his flat brow.

"Gary, calm yourself and remember your station. I voiced my opinion vigorously. I promise you I did. But the entire council decided. I did what I could do. And believe me, they know I am upset," Gary's uncle Paulo explained.

"You're upset? What about me? I've trained my whole life for this trip, and now they are going back to Earth without me. I'm way more qualified than most of the people chosen."

Paulo gave Gary a sideways glance at this statement. His nephew was smart, but those chosen were at the top of their fields as well.

"Did you even complain about that idiot Flynn attacking me? I can barely lift my arm. My chest hurts, and I could have internal injuries." Gary whined.

Paulo cringed. "Nephew, I tried. But Walker painted a slightly different picture than you did. It was my word versus his."

"And they decided you were the liar?" Gary screamed, spittle flying from his mouth.

"Not fair," Paulo growled. The elder Sanchez was now losing his patience.

Gary gritted his teeth before dropping his gaze to the ground. The look from his uncle was quickly turning away from compassion, and he could sense that. "Yeah, sorry. It's just that our house has no one going on this trip that can represent us. The council has forgotten that you were a key member of the team that arranged this trip. It just isn't fair."

"You must remember one thing, Gary. If this trip is successful, other trips are planned. You will eventually be selected," Paulo said, trying to remain upbeat and positive.

"Maybe. But I'm not sure if I'm willing to wait 'til next time."

"What does that mean? Please, do not do something we both will regret," Paulo said adamantly.

With a face that had gone stone cold, Gary Sanchez glowered at his uncle. His jaws tightened and his brow furrowed, and it looked to his uncle as if his nephew was going to have internal combustion and burst into flames. Suddenly, without another word, the overgrown boy of a man balled up his fists and stormed out.

****

Melanie and Flynn arrived at the Spaceport Terminal the next morning at 5 a.m. Only twenty-eight hours remained before the M453-E would depart from its current Mars orbit. The crew milled about the shuttle launch area as they said goodbye to family and friends. Each team member had a special someone to say goodbye to and received hugs and kisses, accompanied by random tears and laughter. But there were also hundreds of other well-wishers that had filled the area. Martians from all sectors of the planet had come to wish them bon voyage. It was an extraordinary moment, a historical moment, and it was being embraced and enjoyed by all–all except for one.

That concealed individual paid no heed to the revelry. Darkly clad, the obscure figure moved low and in a serpentine manner, slithering snakelike as he moved between various crates and provisions still waiting to be loaded on the last shuttle run. After darting in and out of the shadows, he finally made his way to a spot close to the shuttle's ramp. He stooped low, hid behind two large boxes, and waited for his moment.

His breath labored and sweat poured down his face as he eyed the dock crew packing the remaining items for the voyage. When no one was watching, he planned to race onboard and conceal himself among the outgoing crates. He might not have been chosen by the group of hypocrites and false Martian leaders to go on the mission, but by God—invited or not—a Sanchez would be going. This expedition could be a once-in-a-lifetime trip, and he would not be left behind.

Michael Walker arrived with every other member of the Council. Though many still felt trepidation about the journey, they wanted to show confidence and support the crew. Walker mingled and spoke to many before walking up to Flynn.

Taking the young captain's hand in his, he said with sincere admiration, "Flynn, I am so proud. You and your crew have all trained so hard, and it shows. I have marveled at the coordination and expert organization of your troops during this process. And now, it is finally time to go. I have to admit that few of us thought this event would ever occur." Leaning over and whispering, Walker added, "A part of me wishes I were going too. To see our home planet would be, well, life-altering."

"There's room for one more," Flynn said, a caring smile on his face.

"And don't think I hadn't thought about taking that space. But, frankly, I couldn't see a single council member not wanting to go on this trip. And that's where things would get dicey; who would go and who would not? Look at what happened to Mr. Sanchez. No, we decided only you and your crew would go—this time," Walker said with a wink.

"Would have loved to have you along, sir," Flynn said with genuine affection.

As they continued to talk, Flynn caught movement out of the corner of his eye. *Had he seen someone running through the shadows toward the loading area to the shuttle?*

"Did you see that?" Flynn asked Walker as he stepped toward the movement.

"See what?"

"I think someone just ran into the loading bay of the shuttle." Flynn focused on the area around the bay doors of the ship.

"No, I didn't see anything. You probably just saw one of the loading crew," Walker assured.

"Of course. Though. . ." Flynn stopped and considered. "I think I'll check just in case."

As Flynn started toward the shuttle's cargo hold, Melanie called to him, "Flynn, look who's here."

Flynn turned to see Marc Antony arriving with mission control commander, Buddy Tyler.

"M.A., what's going on?" Flynn asked the droid.

"I'm not exactly sure. I received an electronic summons by Commander Tyler with instructions to gather extra supplies for myself and meet him here," Marc Antony answered.

Flynn shot a quizzical gaze at Walker and then at Tyler. "What's going on?" he repeated.

Walker shook his head unknowingly, but Tyler spoke up. "Mission control planners deliberated last night and decided to add a droid to the crew. We believe Marc Antony to be an ideal selection, as your unit is one of the most advanced models on the planet. Not to mention the fact that both you and Ms. Canfield are now going on the mission, which freed your droid from its regular duties. So, we summoned him right after the two of you left your home this morning. Once he arrived, I downloaded some additional data about the trip and, here he is."

"Figures. And here I thought we'd finally received a break from him for a few months." Flynn grinned.

"Oh, I get it, humor. HA. . .HA. . .HA. . ." Marc Antony groaned with a fake laugh.

"Sarcasm, very good M.A.," Melanie said.

"Thank you, Melanie," Marc Antony answered, pleased and proud.

"Yeah, whatever," Flynn grumbled good-naturedly.

An alarm on Flynn's watch went off, alerting him of the impending departure time. He sent M.A. to advise the crew to board the shuttle. One by one, they said their last goodbyes and entered the transport. Flynn was the last to walk up the gangway. Just as he got to the ship's threshold, he took a sideways glance toward the loading dock. His eyes narrowed. He considered Walker's reply regarding the shadowy figure Flynn thought he'd seen. Unable to let it go, he went to check things out.

As Flynn headed toward the rear of the ship, Melanie called out, "Hey captain, are you going AWOL?"

"Not on your life. Just want to check on something. They can retrieve the gangway. I'll enter the ship from the cargo hold," Flynn said as he jogged toward the loading area.

Moving along the back wall of a darkened patch of the shuttle storage hold, Gary Sanchez smiled like a child with a new toy. He believed he'd made it on board unnoticed, and he was reveling in that success. Now, he just needed to hold on and wait. Once the shuttle left the planet and made its way to the spaceship, he would execute his next move; sneak on board the M453-E and find a hiding place 'till the ship left orbit. Even if he was eventually discovered, Everett wouldn't turn around to take him back. At that moment, a tall, muscular figure entered the now darkened shuttle storage area.

"Lights on," a voice said. It was Flynn Everett.

The hidden man froze. Not because the slightest movement or noise might give his hiding spot away, it was because he was stiffened by fright. Flynn wouldn't hesitate to throttle him if he were caught. Hell, as volatile as he was, the man might even kill him.

The spaceship captain dashed up the ramp, scanning the area and looking for what or who he didn't know. The loading crew had exited the craft, and the bay hold was only half full of last-minute provisions. This area appeared normal and vacant of anyone—but something didn't feel right. For some reason, Flynn's internal alarms were banging loud and long.

With cautious curiosity, he made his way around a few large crates, looking over and around their storage locations. Each glance produced a pang of adrenal anticipation. Yet, the searches produced nothing. As he was about to circle around the last crate, a profound, non-deliberate tensing of his muscles occurred. There was a space of about two and a half feet between the crate and the back corner of the storage area. A perfect spot for anyone trying to hide. The last spot, in fact. He put his hand on the top of the metal box and began to step around. . .

Melanie's voice on the com-link broke Everett's focus. "Flynn let's go. We'll be behind schedule if you don't come now."

****

Possibly as scared as he had ever been in his life, Gary Sanchez knew Everett was inches away from discovering his hiding spot. He knew if he moved backward a couple of feet, and then slid sideways, he could get to a spot that he might not be seen. But Sanchez was still frozen in place by sheer panic. Flynn was now directly on the other side of the box he hid behind. Only a matter of inches separated him from certain discovery, and that's when he heard Melanie Canfield's voice alerting Flynn of his potential tardiness.

Flynn turned toward the loading dock entryway and tapped his com-link. "Yeah, coming. Just need to check one more thing. Be there in a sec."

This momentary distraction gave Sanchez his chance. Like a startled rat that sees a hole to escape, he slid back and to his left several feet. He was now no longer in direct view of his previous hiding spot.

From this new position, the unnerved man watched through the shadows as Everett checked the very spot where he had just been. Sanchez's heart slammed in his chest, and his hands trembled so badly that he thought the bones inside would rattle. And though the air temperature was a cool seventy degrees, little rivulets of fear-induced sweat poured down his face.

Flynn frowned as the last spot anyone could hide was empty. He was still uncomfortable with the image he'd seen earlier but shook it off and made his way inside the shuttle to the passenger's cabin. A bone-chilling alarm echoed throughout the area, and the cargo doors closed with a vacuum-sealing thrum. Ten minutes later, the crowd outside the shuttle had moved to the safety of the observation area as the crew inside strapped themselves into their seats and awaited the shuttle's lift-off. Flynn glanced at each of those onboard and then at Melanie. "No turning back now. How do you feel?" he asked.

"Not necessarily. I could stay right where I am and come back on the return shuttle trip," Melanie chortled. "Just kidding. Actually, I feel remarkably calm. I thought I'd have butterflies, but I have none."

"Wait 'til we're on board the M453-E when the thrusters kick in and we slingshot around the planet towards Earth. The butterflies will flap their wings like hummingbirds."

"Looking forward to it!"

In the shuttle's cargo hold, Gary Sanchez reveled in his success. And though he'd almost been caught, and it scared the hell out of him, it was also one of the most thrilling moments of personal victory he'd ever known. Giving the golden boy Everett the slip was exhilarating. He couldn't wait to throw it in his face. Everything was going as planned.

The rumbling of the shuttle's engines coming to life seconds later startled Sanchez out of his moment of gloating. He stiffened in a panic until he realized what was happening. Gathering his wits, he leaned back against the wall, placed his feet against the nearest crate, and hung on.

As he sat and waited, basking in his victory, Sanchez's mind began wrapping around the reality of what was to come next. Suddenly, like a freight train hitting him head-on, he realized that sneaking on the main spaceship was going to be much more difficult.

The cover of darkness was his ally when he crept onto the shuttle. But things would be quite different once the shuttle docked with the M453-E. His recent thrill of victory vanished and was replaced by another bout of paralyzing fear. What was he thinking? He trembled, and a fresh round of sweat began coating his face.

****

The passengers of the last shuttle going to the M453-E heard the final alert and braced themselves. The electronic shield was disengaged, there was no permanent shielding in this area, and the thrusters of the vessel were initiated. Within several seconds, the transport lifted off and headed skyward. Thirty minutes later, the craft docked with the M453-E.

Once the docking bay was secured and sealed, the last members of the crew that were due onboard disembarked. Flynn and

Melanie walked to a lift station where they exchanged a light kiss and headed in opposite directions; Flynn to the bridge, while Melanie went to the science command center.

At that moment, the cargo bay of the shuttle opened, and crewmen prepared to unload the last-minute provisions before the shuttle went back to the planet's surface. Gary Sanchez, a non-registered piece of cargo, was frozen in place, hidden behind a crate at the far side of the cargo hold. He could hear voices of the M453-E's crew milling about, only 15 meters from where he sat. He considered, at that moment, to spring up and surrender. His internal fortitude had evaporated as fear had erased his desired purpose and plans. But just before he was about to stand up, fate stepped in.

"There appear to be a few more crates than I thought there were going to be," a man's voice said. "We'll have to move a few provisions from that far wall so we can get these stowed. Ben, Joe, come with me and we'll get that done. Clay, you loosen the bindings on these boxes. Once we make room, we'll come with a moving module and transfer these to the ship."

"Yes sir," a voice responded.

Sanchez heard footsteps move off, and then a pair heading toward where he was. He somehow regained his composure and slid around the crate he hid behind and glimpsed the crewman coming into the shuttle. A stocky man, with broad shoulders from years of heaving heavy materials, casually walked right past where Sanchez lay in wait and began removing straps from boxes in the far corner of the hold.

Moving as quietly as he could, Sanchez crawled along a narrow pathway till he made it to the shuttle bay door. He could hear the other men's voices and movement of boxes and such from the far side of the spaceship's cargo bay but could see no one.

Glancing once more at the crewman onboard the shuttle, Sanchez took in a deep breath, made his choice, then bolted for a spot behind two large metal crates onboard the M453-E to his right. As he scooted along the deck, he spotted the top of a man's head as it turned a corner to his left. The person was heading down a path that would put the deckhand directly in line to where Sanchez had decided would be his new hiding spot.

Doubling his effort, Sanchez made a last-second jolt to his right, then dove along the ground, propelling himself to the crate closest to him. Once he got his body past the edge of the crate, he rolled over while simultaneously pulling in his legs just as the loading dock worker passed the last crate. He was manipulating a hovering moving module, appearing not to have seen Sanchez's flight. *Another brilliant victory*, Sanchez thought.

Chapter 9

Moving toward the bridge lift, Everett stopped several times to speak to various crew members as they finished last-minute details for the ship's departure. His team seemed understandably on edge. It had taken three-plus years to prepare for this moment, and though he believed they were ready, he could feel the buzzing apprehension.

Seeing the level-3 station commander, Flynn stopped him mid-stride. "What's the mood, Dean?"

"All good and ship-shape, Captain," Commander Dean Cooper snapped in reply.

"Off the record?" Flynn queried.

Dean looked past the captain towards a small group of workers. "I might respond nervous and anxious if I thought it accurate. But to be honest, I am sensing excitement and enthusiasm. They're doing their jobs, doing them well, and enjoying every aspect of the moment. It is a joy to behold. Couldn't be prouder, sir."

"Good to hear. I must admit to feeling the same way," Flynn said, smiling.

"Right back at you, sir."

"Carry on," Flynn said, and the two saluted each other. As Everett walked away, he glanced back at the crewmen at work. He wondered how their faces would change as the ship made its slingshot maneuver around Mars. He doubted there would be many that would find the ride so exciting, exhilarating, or for that matter, very much fun.

Positioned around the M453-E spaceship were four lift stations. One for each of the "primary" work areas, and one leading to the crew's quarters and living areas. Flynn approached the lift that serviced the bridge. The door slid sideways, allowing him entry. He stepped in, and the door closed behind him with a soft whir. "Bridge," Flynn ordered. Though Everett had yet to make it to his appointed station, the staff already knew of his impending arrival to the bridge.

The Captain's chair, as programmed, had announced his appearance once Flynn stepped onto the ship. The spacecraft fleet on Mars were equipped with 'Interactive DNA Captain's Chairs.' Though others might need to pilot the ship, the chair, and its internal DNA matching code, gave the captain access to certain commands that only he could use. These highly advanced seats only "activated" once sensors detected the Captain's presence.

"Captain on the bridge," Lt. Cummings said as the lift door opened. Everyone immediately stood at attention as their young leader came into the chamber.

The M453-E's Bridge was oval shaped, measuring twenty-five meters by twenty meters. From the center of the bridge, which rose to twelve meters, the ceiling sloped down to ten meters along the perimeter. There was an exterior viewing screen made of the same transparent material as the shields covering the Martian settlements. The screen possessed a tensile strength like Martian tungsten/enamel and could withstand similar impacts that the hull could handle. However, in extreme situations, a high-energy electronic shield could be engaged to cover the area with additional protection.

The bridge housed various workstations and status panels. Most of the ship's functions were controlled from these areas, though other sectors of the ship could provide backup functionality if needed. The captain's chair was about two-thirds back from the viewing screen in the middle of the room.

To the seat's right were the pilot and navigator stations, and to the left was the second in command's position and an engineering station. A 3D Virtual Status Imagery System was in front of the captain's chair and directly under the highest point of the room. This instrument provided instant access to any data in the ship's information servers and a 3D version of all communications between those onboard or those with similar broadcast capabilities.

"As you were," Flynn responded to the group's concerted action. "Status?"

"All pre-flight testing checked out with only one minor issue," Second-in-command Bert Parker said.

Flynn swiveled his seat to look at Parker. "And that would be?"

"During our most updated pre-flight systems analysis, a sensor detected an unaccountable weight variance of 130 kilograms."

"The source?"

"Well, that's the thing. We could not locate the origin of the discrepancy. We accounted for the last provisions that came on board on the last shuttle," Parker said.

"That weight's roughly the size of one of our crew members. Is the personnel manifest downloaded properly into the weight configurations?" Everett asked.

"Yes sir, right down to the last person who boarded today—you sir."

Flynn sat silent for a moment. That same feeling that something wasn't right returned. He couldn't help thinking about the cargo bay incident before they'd left the planet's surface. Someone could have tried to get on the ship for the mission. But to sneak on without being detected, especially with the ship's advanced sensor systems, seemed highly unlikely. And for what purpose? The undertaking had its detractors, but maybe a saboteur?

"Mr. Parker, instruct Ensign Barnes and Ensign Navin to do a thorough search of the cargo bay. Top to bottom, and all crates and packages large enough to conceal a person," Flynn instructed.

"You think we have a stowaway on board?"

"Not sure. But as a precaution, let's give the area a good going over. Don't announce the order over your com-link to Barnes and Navin. Have the two report to you for instructions."

Parker touched his com-link twice and waited. After a moment, he said, "Ensign Barnes and Navin, report to the Bridge.

Chapter 10

Officially an M453-E stowaway, Gary Sanchez sat in nervous apprehension. He had successfully made it from the shuttle to the M453-E without being caught. A victory that seemed far-fetched at best only a few minutes before. Once again, it had been a close call, with his nerves pushing him to the brink of throwing up.

But now he was once again giddy with anticipation of going to Earth. Yet, to be free of the fear of being discovered before he was ready, he determined the need for a better hiding place. Moments later, he found what he was looking for. The internal access shafts of the ship. A perfect place to hide, he thought.

Sanchez made his way to an internal systems access panel on the far side of the bay. He chose this location as it was the farthest access portal from the entry of the cargo bay as it could be. Less chance of being heard or seen.

There were two latches at the bottom of the panel. He easily loosened the left latch and released it from its cradle. He focused next on the right side, but the winged latch there seemed welded in place. "Come on, damn you," Sanchez said through gritted teeth. He spent several agonizing minutes trying to no avail. He gave up. There must be other panels along this wall. He hunted for another access panel, moving in and around stored supplies and provisions, but there were no others on this side of the bay. As he began to head to another wall, the cargo bay door slid open.

"So, they think a stowaway snuck onboard. Boy, can you imagine the nerve you must have to try that?" Ensign Navin said as the two crewmen entered the hold.

"Keep your voice down, Joe; you heard what Parker said. If an unauthorized person is on the ship somewhere, we don't want to announce we know it," Barnes chastised.

"Okay, sorry," Navin winced as he realized his blunder.

"You search around the perimeter to your left, and I'll do the right. We'll meet in the middle of the back wall then work our way back through the center," Barnes instructed.

Ordered by Parker to carry weapons, the two men removed stun wands from the sheaths at their waist.

When Sanchez heard the word "stowaway," he almost gasped out loud. How did they know? He raced back to the previous access panel and began working on the stuck latch again. If he didn't get it open, he was done. Footfalls were echoing around the hold, making it impossible for Sanchez to know how close the men were or even which direction they were going. He knew that he was running out of time. If he didn't get that latch opened, he'd have to try to evade their search by skittering around boxes as they searched. Not being seen or heard doing that would be a long shot. He gave the handle the last ounce of strength he had… and the latch turned.

With trembling hands, Sanchez quickly loosened the latch the rest of the way, opened the access panel, and crawled inside before softly closing the panel. He made it... at least he thought he had until a stark realization hit him. If one of his pursuers saw the two bottom locks hanging loose, they would do a thorough search inside the shaft.

Sanchez could see a slit running across the bottom of the panel. It was a tight squeeze, but if he could manage to slip his fingers through and lift the latches back to their positions? No way he could tighten them, but if they were in their cradles, maybe the searchers wouldn't notice. He fumbled around a few times until he finally snagged the first latch, pushed the piece of metal up, and secured it. As he suspected, he couldn't tighten it.

Sanchez pulled his fingers back and then shifted his attention to the second latch. This proved more difficult. He couldn't use his right hand, the angle was wrong, and he wasn't as coordinated with his left. After making several attempts but couldn't get the latch in its cradle. He swore under his breath, listened for footsteps, and tried one last time. The latch momentarily caught and then fell back with a small clang. At that moment, he heard a shuffling sound and knew someone was close. He pulled his fingers back just as ensign Navin turned down the aisleway.

****

Supply crates and containers sat in almost every conceivable space in the hold and were secured to the walls, the ceiling, and the floor by various harnesses and strappings. A few aisles remained clear to allow admittance to the access panels leading to the internal workings of the ship in that sector. Convinced the whole stowaway story to be a farce, Ensign Navin gave little effort to the search, only glanced here and there. At the panel where Sanchez was hidden, Navin almost turned a blind eye. But, by chance, he happened a glance down.

"Hmm," the ensign mused. He leaned down and tried the right latch– it was loose. "Barnes, over here," he called out.

77

"I'm on my way," Barnes replied.

Barnes ran up the center of the cargo bay until he got to the aisle where Navin stood.

"What did you find?" Barnes asked.

"Not sure. Maybe nothing. But check this out. The latch on the right is on, though I've checked it and it's loose. And the one on the left is hanging down unattached."

"There's no way that was like that before. Let's open it," Barnes said, his stun wand at the ready.

Navin snorted, still baffled by anyone thinking they could sneak on board, and then pulled down the latch on the right. Both latches now hung open. He glanced up at Barnes, nodded, and slowly lifted the access panel.

"Access shaft number twenty-three. Lights on," Navin said. The lights came on inside the crawl space. "Oh shit," Navin blurted.

"What! What's there?" Barnes stuttered as he took a step back.

"MY GOD," Navin shouted, then broke into a laugh. "There's nothing here! The shaft is empty all the way to the end."

"You can be such a jerk. You're lucky I don't shove this wand up your ass," Barnes swore before tapping his com-link. "Captain Everett?" he said.

"This is the Captain."

"Captain, the access panel to access shaft number twenty-three was not secured. One latch was attached but loose, and the other hung completely off. We opened the panel but found nothing."

Everett thought for a moment and then said, "Secure the grate and return to your stations. Captain out."

"I know that look." Brad Cummings said as he glanced toward Flynn.

"I'm sure it's nothing, but…" Flynn replied.

"But?"

Flynn considered the situation. "Never mind. As I said, I'm sure it's nothing."

Staring out of the bridge's viewscreen, Flynn considered the possibilities of who and why someone might have snuck on board. He thought back to Gary Sanchez's warning, but just as quickly discounted the man as too much of a coward to attempt such a feat. After a few minutes more of contemplation, he tapped his com-link twice, giving him access to the entire crew.

"This is the Captain. In twelve hours, we will be leaving the only home any of us have ever known. And yet, we will be going to our founding father's place of birth. This is an exciting prospect, to say the least. Yet, it is important to understand that the planet may not be the same as it was when the original Mars flight left Earth, and not what we all hope it will be. Despite that, we go with a purpose and a plan. Throughout the journey, we must never forget that our families, our friends, and the rest of the populace on Mars are depending on us to do our jobs and to come home safely.

"At 09:00 tomorrow, we will be in the correct position for the ship to accelerate towards a slingshot trajectory around Mars. This alternative path will allow us to arrive at Earth's atmosphere within 62/Mars days, well ahead of our original arrival schedule. However, I want to remind you that this procedure will create a significant G-force. We have taken this into account and know our craft will withstand anything thrown its way. And though the ship will meet all challenges, your responsibility is to be harnessed at your posts so that you can do your jobs without fear of injury.

"Everyone on this ship has an essential function throughout each phase of our mission. From this chair, I have no doubt each of us will execute those responsibilities to the highest levels. Finally, thank you all for the hard work and dedication to date. I am proud of all of you, as I have observed a genuine commitment to seeing this mission succeed. Captain out."

****

Gary Sanchez lowered himself down from access shaft twenty-four into access shaft twenty-three. He had eluded capture once again. He was getting pretty good at this hide-and-seek game. With all lights off, the shaft was pitch-black. He reached into a small slit in his sleeve and pulled out a pencil thin flashlight and switched it on. He then retraced his steps back to the access panel where he had entered the shaft and tried to move it.

"Shit. Shit, shit, shit," Sanchez swore. The men had re-tightened the latches. He stepped back and used his small light to look around. The beam shone on a conglomerate of pipes, and conduits, but nothing of use to help him get out. He reasoned he could stay in the shaft for a while, but he would have to get out—eventually. But how? A single bead of sweat appeared at his left scalp line and ran down his face. Soon, nervous tension produced the salty fluid lines in steady streams. His earlier fear of being found had turned into terror of *not* being found and dying of dehydration and starvation. Why hadn't he thought to bring at least a little food?

Shining the light down the shaft, he crawled its length until he made it back to the far end. Once there, he found an access passageway heading both to his right and left. He shined his beam one way, stared into the void for several moments, and then turned the beam the other way. Both shafts appeared identical. Attached to the walls and ceiling were multitudes more of the same kinds of pipes and wiring conduits. He shook his head and closed his eyes. He hadn't counted on being trapped in one of the shafts. And he certainly didn't believe he'd be found out so soon? *But how could it be? No way Everett could know it was him, no way!* After a moment, he moved the beam of light down the shaft to his left and crawled.

****

Flynn met Melanie in the ship's dining hall, and the two sat with several members of the senior staff for dinner. Most everyone at the table glowed with energy and excitement, and the lively conversations centered on different perspectives regarding the trip ahead. But eventually, someone asked Flynn the question everyone wanted to ask.

"So, Captain," a young engineering officer started. "What if we arrive there, and?" The woman paused.

"And things aren't so good?" Flynn offered.

"What if everyone is dead?" she added.

"Let's hope that's not the case. But if it is, then we will assess the planet's life support capabilities and return home with our findings."

81

Several long beats of silence hung in the air like a hangman's noose. Finally, Melanie broke the awkward silence by raising her glass of wine. "Here's to getting to Earth, finding a planet full of life, and returning home safely!"

The group all raised their glasses to the toast and echoed her sentiments.

Chapter 11

08:34

The Bridge of the M475-E

"Mr. Cummings, status?" Flynn asked as he stared out of the bridge's viewing screen.

"We are roughly 15,000 kilometers from Mars' gravitational field. Current speed is 42,500 kilometers per hour. We should contact the field's outer edge in about 6 minutes."

Flynn double tapped his com-link. "This is the Captain. In approximately five minutes, we will start the slingshot maneuver. I want everyone in their safety positions. Those at standing stations must be in their protective harnesses. It's going to be a rough ride while we're in the throes of Mars' gravity. Also, as we leave orbit, the ship will experience some momentary but intense turbulence. Under no circumstances do I want our doctor to report that any of my crew was injured from not being properly secured. Captain out."

"One-minute-forty-five," Cummings alerted.

"At fifteen seconds, initiate the warning alarm," Flynn replied.

"Yes, sir."

Flynn watched as the ship approached Mars. The planet began filling the ship's viewing screen; its mass blocking out two-thirds of the display. Flynn sensed a slight vibration in his command chair. "Here we go," he muttered just as the alarm sounded.

At first, the vibration was minimal—just a minor tremor. Then, as the M-453-E dove into the planet's gravitational field at almost 43,000 kilometers per hour, the slight tremor turned into a steady shake. This shuddering soon morphed into a g-force quake that shook the ship as if the vessel was in a paint-mixing machine.

Flynn looked around the bridge. Each crew member seemed focused on his or her respective tasks with furrowed brows that displayed intense concentration. His staff traveled extensively around the planet during training, but no one, not even the most seasoned crewman, had been through a slingshot maneuver. Even so, Everett sensed no outward emotional evidence of fear on anyone's face.

"Five minutes till gravitational exit," Cummings announced in a staccato fashion.

As the ship's rumbling continued at a fevered pitch, Flynn felt adrenalin pumping through his body. He glanced down and saw that he had a white-knuckled grip on his chair, and the veins on his arms were bulging. He sensed that his tendons and muscles were contracted to their fullest, and he was gritting, no, gnashing his teeth. All signs that he was experiencing a highly stressful situation. But all the while, he had a huge smile on his face.

"Really?" Cummings said as he glanced toward his friend and captain.

"Yeah, great right?" Flynn replied. He'd done all the calculations, though they were at times theoretical–the results were playing out. He was thrilled.

"Yeah, great," Cummings said in a vibration altered stutter, and with much less enthusiasm.

Throughout the ship, the emotions of the moment by the crew varied widely. Those at active stations went about their assignments without fail. Non-active crewmen were harnessed and holding fast, though some, like twenty-six-year-old janitorial staff member Lester Baker, gritted back the urge to scream—or vomit. He was scared and was barely holding it together. It felt to him like every bone in his body was being shaken apart.

"Brace for the gravitational exit," Flynn announced. The ongoing vibrations that the craft had been experiencing shot up to a frightening intensity before the craft slid hard to the left and then whiplashed back to the right. A few storage bins flew open, and unrestrained objects were thrown out and tossed about with ferocious power and velocity.

Then, just as harsh as the exit from Mars' gravitational field was, the rumbling ship smoothed out. It was a stunning transformation and Flynn sensed an immediate change in everyone's bearing. All seemed back to normal, yet now the ship was humming along at roughly 75,000 kilometers per hour.

"Mr. Parks?" Everett queried.

Second-in-command Parks sat like a mute for several long moments as he tapped multiple icons on his workstation console. The bridge crew stared at the twirling three-D sensory system that materialized in the center of the bridge. The informational data, previously projecting the ship's slingshot path around Mars, had now morphed into a column of damage control information. Dozens of green lights showed that most of the ship survived the maneuver with little or no issue. However, a lone red light blinked repeatedly in the center of the projection.

Flynn noticed the irregularity. "Mr. Parks?".

"I see it, Captain," Parks replied. He touched his screen a few more times, and an image of an access passageway appeared. "It is in electrical shaft number twenty-three, between corridor six and seven. It seems that a relay station has malfunctioned. The shaft is accessed from the cargo hold." Without command, Parks tapped his com-link. "Ensign Navin and Barnes—" Before he could finish, Flynn held up his hand.

"Instruct them to meet me at the level three, lift station number nine," Flynn instructed as he hopped up from his seat.

"Sir?" Parks asked in surprise.

"Thank you, Mr. Parks," Flynn acknowledged without another word of explanation. Flynn stepped into the bridge lift and headed down to the third level. He made his way to station number nine, where Ensign Navin and Barnes awaited.

"Captain, is there something wrong?" Navin asked as Flynn approached.

"Probably not. Just a hunch that I prefer to check for myself," Flynn answered as he sped past the two security officers.

"Yes sir," Ensign Navin said as he and Barnes hurried to keep up with the fast-paced Flynn. "Mr. Parks said shaft twenty-three. The same access corridor we searched before?"

Flynn nodded in acknowledgment as the three headed to the cargo bay. They made their way to shaft twenty-three's access panel. Barnes loosened the panel's latches.

<hr>

"Shaft twenty-three, lights on," Flynn said as he entered the shaft. The lights along the shaft's length illuminated the area.

Navin looked at his info-pad, and said, "The sensor is down around fifteen meters near the junction of corridors six and seven,"

"Yes," Flynn agreed. He tapped his com-link once and said, "Doctor Carlson?"

There was a moment of silence and then, "Carlson here."

"Doctor, come to the cargo hold, we have an injury in Shaft number twenty-three near corridor six and seven. I think you will need a hover-stretcher," Flynn said.

There was silence for another moment and then the ship's doctor said, "I'm not showing any issues with any member of our crew, Captain. All life support identifications show the crew to be well and at their respective stations or in their quarters."

"Yes, I think an extra passenger found their way on board."

Navin and Barnes looked at each other and then at their captain. Flynn nodded toward the end of the shaft. Sticking out at the crossing of corridors number six and seven–was a foot.

****

"You have got to be kidding. Sanchez?" Melanie said, shocked.

"Yep. He's a bit messed up, too. Doc says he suffered a broken left leg and right arm. He has bumps and bruises all over his body and several lacerations. I'm going to meet with him in thirty minutes; want to join?"

"You bet," Melanie replied. After a moment more of thought, she said, "You know what, I think I'll pass. No doubt he will be staying with us for the duration of the flight–"

"Unless I jettison him off the ship in a life pod," Flynn interjected.

"Yes, as I was saying, he's going to be with us for a while, so I think I'll skip the temptation to ridicule and chastise. If he's messed up as bad as you say, I would feel guilty giving him grief right now."

"Suit yourself. But just so you know, I plan on grilling the jerk unmercifully," Flynn warned with a chuckle.

"Yeah. And Sanchez deserves it. But maybe you'll want to cut him a little slack till he recovers?" There was an obvious if not deliberate silence from Flynn and then Melanie sighed in resignation, "I guess not."

"Nope. I'm afraid it's the third degree for my friend Gary Sanchez. I'll catch up with you at dinner and fill you in on how it went. Flynn out."

Thirty minutes later, the Captain entered the sick bay. "Hey Doc, how's the patient?"

"Oh, my. You know, Mr. Sanchez is lucky to have just a couple of broken bones. He could have easily cracked his skull open and died before anybody knew he was on board," Carlson responded with genuine concern.

"Think of the smell. . .sorry, bad joke." Flynn grimaced as he caught the older man's glare. "What I meant to say was, boy, he is lucky. So, can I talk to him?"

"Yes. But Mr. Sanchez is a bit loopy from the pain meds I gave him. He may not be totally on top of the conversation."

"He better clear the cobwebs out because I'm not happy," Flynn warned. The captain made his way past the doctor's lab and into the recovery area where Gary Sanchez lay. Per Flynn's explicit instructions, Sanchez was secured via safety straps. He was conscious and staring up at the ceiling. "Doctor Smith?" Flynn said as he walked up to the restrained Sanchez."

"What? Who?" Sanchez said as he turned his head toward Flynn.

"Come on—you know, Doctor Smith? From the Lost in Space television series from Earth? Everybody remembers him. From the Historical Archives viewing series? Yes?" Flynn said with a broad smile on his face.

Sanchez looked confused.

"No, huh? That's a shame because that guy really cracked me up. Couldn't trust him for anything. A total coward. Reminds me of somebody we both know."

"Spare me your sophomoric attempts at humor. Don't you realize I'm injured?" Sanchez whined as he turned his head away.

"Yeah, too bad about that. But guess what? You'll have plenty of time to recover. By the time we arrive on Earth, you'll be good as new. Just as out of shape and unconditioned as when you snuck on board. But you know what, since you'll be in your quarters the entire trip, it won't matter to you. One good note though, you will be provided with three meals a day, so it won't be a total loss. And to that point, since we have roughly two months of flight time before we get to Earth, what were you going to eat the whole time? Did you plan just to show up at the mess and eat there, or order in?"

Sanchez started to speak, but Everett held up a hand. "Gary, what were you thinking? Did you expect to sneak on my ship and be welcomed with open arms? Whatever your ignorant brain was contemplating, just know that you will be placed under arrest and kept that way until we return to Mars. Once there, I will personally make sure you receive everything coming to you."

Sanchez had been looking away, but at this statement, he jerked toward Flynn. "You can't be serious? Do you realize who my family is? You won't get away with it," Sanchez warned.

"You might be right about that." Flynn rubbed at his chin and then added with conviction, "Probably should skip all the drama and just stuff you in a life pod and jettison you out into space. Save a lot of headaches for me, that's for sure. But hey, don't worry, the self-guided pod would get you back to Mars, eventually. . .probably." Flynn said.

"Hilarious, ha, ha, ha!" Sanchez scoffed.

"Yeah, that would be funny," Flynn agreed. "Need to put some thought into a best-case worst-case scenario on that one. In the meantime, you will stay here, restrained, until the Doc says you can be moved. Once you are well enough, you will be taken to guarded quarters until I decide whether to keep you there or jettison your ass back to Mars. Good talk, Mr. Sanchez. I hope you enjoy the ride." With that, Flynn walked out, leaving Sanchez with his mouth open in stunned disbelief. As he passed Doctor Carlson, Flynn smiled and winked. The doctor frowned and shook his head.

Chapter 12

Earth – the year 2355

Boulderside Colony

Rocky Mountains—Colorado

"Are ya sure," Tate asked the young man seated at the radio controls.

"No doubt. I change the frequencies at least twice a week. Today, this mornin' in fact, I went to my third pre-set signal point and picked this up," the radioman said. He turned a couple of dials, and then a huge smile crossed his face. "See, isn't it amazin'?"

Tate stared down at Bobby Hammonds, the resident radioman, and then shrugged his shoulders.

At first, Hammonds was disappointed in Tate's lack of excitement, and then he understood. "Oh, sorry," Bobby said. He grimaced in embarrassment before pulling his headphones plug out of the receiver port. A voice immediately came on:

"People of Earth. My name is Captain Flynn Everett of the M453-E Star Ship. We have traveled from Mars and wish to contact those currently in charge of Earth's governing bodies. Our crew is comprised of direct descendants of the original space travelers sent to Mars from Earth almost 300 Earth years ago. If you are receiving this message, and can respond, please give us your coordinates so we may pinpoint your location. We will be arriving in Earth's atmosphere in approximately five Earth days."

Tate's eyes went huge, his mouth flopped open, and he seemed cemented in place. As the radioman beamed in triumph, Tate blinked and took in a breath for the first time since the communication started.

"I think it's a looped recordin'. The message gets repeated every 10 minutes and changes frequencies about every two hours," Bobby said in excitement.

"Who else knows about this?" Tate asked.

"Only Pam. She was with me when I heard the transmission the first time."

"Where is she, Bobby?" Tate said in a panicked tone.

"She went to the council chamber lookin' for ya," he said as his voice trailed off in knowing apprehension.

"How much longer are we goin' to wait?" an elder barked to the others. "We've been told that Tate was on his way nearly 20 minutes ago."

"Patience," Terry Peters said. But as he did, he could plainly see on the faces around the room that the council's *patience* was quickly vanishing. And with Frank Potter's constant prodding, Peters worried that a decision based on panic and fear would prevail, with or without Tate's input.

Potter sat speaking with a group of anxious listeners before turning toward Peters. A broad triumphant smile crossed his face, and he was about to say something when Pamela Jenkins came running into the chamber.

"Ya won't believe it! Ya won't believe what just happened," she stammered.

"Ms. Jenkins! Ya know better than to come into this room unannounced," Perry Smith scolded. Smith's normally hunched shoulders seemed to straighten as he crowed this declaration.

The girl came to a skidding stop while staring wide-eyed in shock as she realized her mistake. No one was permitted in a council meeting unless properly vetted for introduction by a member beforehand—especially a girl of fifteen.

"Take a breath, Pam, and tell us what's happenin'," Peters said in a fatherly tone.

Pam inhaled deeply, let the breath out in a nervous puff, and tried to speak. Unfortunately, only a squeak came out as her throat had constricted through sheer anxiousness, and the overwhelming significance of the message she was about to give. She squeezed her eyes shut, swallowed hard, shook her head, and blurted, "Bobby got a message from OUTER SPACE!"

Just as the girl shrieked her words, Tate walked in.

****

"What does this mean?

"Is the message real?"

"Who sent whom to Mars 300 years ago?"

These questions and many more were hurtled about by everyone in the room. Chaos and pandemonium reigned as council decorum evaporated.

"Please, please. Just calm down a minute. I'm sure there is a logical explanation for all of this," Terry Peters pleaded, though he looked at Tate in puzzlement. Tate moved to the middle of the room and yelled, "Gentlemen control yarselves and sit down in yar seats - NOW!"

Pam Jenkins jerked at the demand and began inching her way back out of the chamber when Tate grabbed her by the arm. "Stay put," Tate said, eyes blazing.

The girl stood fast, not moving. Even if she wanted to run, she couldn't as it seemed her legs had lost their ability to move.

Though grumbling persisted, the entire council did as Tate directed. Even Frank Potter cowered and moved to his spot, his smug look from moments before now evaporated like hot breath vapors in cold air.

"Now, I understand there are a lot of questions, and I will answer as many as I can. But let me explain to ya what I know beforehand as the story may shed some light," Tate said as he walked over to a raised dais reserved for those with a forum to discuss.

After a heavy exhale, he began, "Most of ya are aware of the historical books and data we possess. All designated leaders of our settlement retain access to this information," Tate said as he nodded towards Terry Peters, the previous head of the colony. "The material contained in the journals mostly speak to Earth's past one hundred to one hundred and fifty years. However, there are a few books that detail history just before the Chinese attacks."

Pam Jenkins, who hadn't moved since Tate froze her with his command, slowly raised her hand.

"I'm sorry Ms. Jenkins. I forgot about ya for a second. Before I allow ya to leave, I'm gonna ask ya to do something that will be difficult for ya to fulfill. I must ask ya to keep the radio message a secret. News like this, well, it might be upsettin' to a lot of our family. So, until we find out the source, its authenticity, and their intentions, ya must keep this to yarself. I have also instructed Bobby Hammonds not to speak of this. It will be hard, and ya will be tempted, but ya must promise not to reveal this news. Can ya do this for me?"

Pam's lips tightened, and her eyes squinted. Tate knew that keeping such a secret was already eating at her, dissolving her reserve like an acid bath. But she nodded yes and said she would obey.

"Good girl. Now go about yar day. I assure ya that ya won't hafta bear this burden for long," Tate said with empathy.

The girl turned on her heels and shuffled out. Reaching the doorway appeared to be a direct signal to her legs to fully function again, and she raced away from the council chamber in a full run.

"Now," Tate said to the men in the room, "In one of the documentations I mentioned, there is detailed information about a one-time secret project to send a group of skilled and educated colonists to Mars.

"It is recorded that 453 people left Earth hopin' to be the catalyst for a new home for our overpopulated planet. Per the documents, the mission progressed as planned. The Earth contingent was well on their way to a successful outpost when all contact was lost. The timin' of this blackout coincided with the Chinese bombing and invasion of several countries—the start of World War Three. No interaction has occurred with those travelers since. At least not as far as documentation in our archives."

"So, this really could be *Earthlin's* arrivin' from Mars?" Dave Kennedy asked from the back of the room.

"I guess so. Or . . ."

"Or what?" Doug Fate, one of the newest council members asked.

"Or it is another group here on Earth tryin' to find us or any other unsuspectin' group," Tate said.

"Come on! This is ridiculous. It's some kind of prank or joke," Frank Potter said as he glared at the council members. "We can't take this seriously. It's a joke or worse. It has to be."

"Maybe," Tate replied, "but, maybe not. What intrigues me is that they claim that they have come from Mars in a spaceship. If'n this is true, what other advancements do they possess? They may have ways to help our colony grow more food. They may even have medicines and cures for a lot of what is wrong here."

"And weapons! Maybe they have ray guns and shit that could help us get rid of the scavengers," Perry Smith gushed with hope.

"Yes, well maybe," Tate said without elaborating on the comment.

"What are ya gonna to do next," Terry Peters calmly asked Tate.

"Try to contact them as soon as I leave here. But until I know exactly who these bein's are and where they are really from, they will not be getting' our coordinates. Even if'n they are who they say they are, I still will not give them our exact location. We will suggest a rendezvous site that will be safe for us. If'n they agree, we will send an envoy to meet them. That's all I have for now. If'n I do make contact and can work thin's out, I will send a runner to all of ya to reconvene."

Frank Potter started to say something, but Tate glowered at him, and he swallowed back the thought. Tate pivoted away and left the room.

****

"Anythin' new?" Tate asked Bobby Hammonds as he entered the radio room.

"Same message, one more time," Bobby said.

Tate sat down next to Bobby. "Ok. Let's try to contact the message sender."

"Really? Wow, this is so awesome!"

"Yeah. I suppose it could be. This is the message I want ya to send," Tate handed the young man a note.

"ME? Ya want *me* to send the message in my voice?" He tapped a pencil against the desk in quick successions.

"Yep. Just say what I've written. Ya'll do fine," Tate smiled, understanding Bobby's nervousness.

"Ok, if'n ya say so. But I'm only a kid, what if'n I screw it up?" Bobby said in a trailing voice. A fatherly smile crossed Tate's face as he nodded for the radioman to give it a try. Hammonds silently read the message to himself and then moved a couple of dials. Clearing his voice, he flipped a switch and began talking into the mike.

Chapter 13

"Captain," Communications Officer Christopher O'Malley called out.

"Mr. O'Malley?" Flynn replied.

"I've got something."

Everett excitedly hopped down from the Captain's chair and moved quickly to O'Malley's side. "Put it on the loudspeaker," Flynn said.

O'Malley tapped two buttons, and a voice streamed through the bridge. "To Captain Everett of the M-453 E spaceship. We are a small colony of humans livin' near the Rocky Mountains. To our knowledge, there are dozens, if'n not more, of small settlements throughout what ya may know as the United States.

"We do not have direct contact with any of those other colonies, nor do we know if'n any survivin' governmental agencies or groups control any larger metropolitan areas. Regardin' a meetin'. We would be excited to have that opportunity. Please contact us at this frequency as soon as ya receive this message. We will be monitorin' our receiver round the clock."

"My God, there are colonies," Flynn said with solemn appreciation.

The rest of the crew took in a collective breath, and then shouts of joy and elation filled the bridge.

Flynn double-tapped his com-link and spoke. "This is the Captain. I am excited to announce that we have received a response to our ongoing communications loop to Earth. However, as we feared, it appears from the contact that the world our ancestors left is not the world we return to. Instead of the cities and vast populations our archives document, there now appears to be only a few colonies left. There are, nevertheless, people on the planet.

"I will share additional information with all of you once we have more detailed conversations. However, I think we can all agree that this is a monumental moment in our quest. Everett out."

Flynn tapped off his com-link. "Mr. O'Malley, do you have the frequency ready?"

"Yes, sir."

"Then let's get them on the line!"

****

Lawrence Tate patted his young radioman on the shoulder. "Ya did very good, Bobby. I'll be in my quarters for a while. Send for me if'n ya hear anythin' at all."

"Yes, sir, Mr. Tate!" Bobby replied.

A squawk and a squeak burst from the radio. "This is Captain Flynn Everett. We have received your message. If you are monitoring your radio now, please respond."

"Holy shit," Bobby Hammonds blurted. "What should I do?"

"Give me the microphone and switch it on," Tate said without hesitation.

Bobby handed Tate the mic and flipped the switch.

Tate swallowed and then said, "This is Lawrence Tate, Governor of Boulderside. Can ya hear me?"

A few pulsating dead air seconds went by before, "Yes, Governor Tate, we can read you loud and clear."

A nervous laugh escaped Tate's mouth. "Captain, I must say, we are a bit surprised to hear from ya. Actually, I think that is a bit of an understatement. We are overwhelmed with excitement. Though there are references to the Mars expedition in some of our history books, we had no way to know if'n the stories were true. So, are ya really from Mars?"

There was static and then, "I'm sure it sounds hard to believe, but yes, we are from Mars. We have a thriving but controlled populace as the original 453 has grown to over 250,000 inhabitants." A few seconds went by, and then Everett added, "Mr. Tate, can I ask what has happened on the Earth. A few short years after our colonists landed on Mars, we lost all communications. We have been fearful that something had occurred that may have decimated the population?"

"Yes, it was written that shortly after the Mars expedition left earth, World War 3 started. But this time, there was no winner as the warrin' governments wiped out most of the entire planet's population. Those that did survive have struggled. For example, our little settlement was established many, many years ago, yet our number here is little mor'n 650.

"Captain, we are very anxious to meet ya. However, and please do not take this the wrong way, but there is a bit of skepticism on our part. There are other groups here on Earth that are, well, shall we say, unscrupulous. They have used ruses on several occasions to brin' us out, and then they attack us."

Flynn looked at Melanie, who had come up to the bridge just moments earlier, and said, "How could that be? Through a purely natural population growth, their numbers should be much higher."

"Agreed. And unscrupulous neighbors that attack them? Earth sounds lovely," Melanie said sarcastically.

Flynn frowned at his science officer and then said, "Understood, Mr. Tate. I am going to guess that none of those groups have spaceships. We will be prepared to arrive in your area in less than 24 hours. If you give us coordinates of a safe landing zone, for you and us, we will set down there. I think the sight of our ship will give you some comfort as to who we are. Is that agreeable?"

****

"Who will go?" Frank Potter asked.

"We will be a party of five. Terry, John Jacobs, Carl Tubbs, me, and of course, ya, Frank," Tate said.

"Me? Really. Oh, thank ya, Larry. It is an honor to represent our colony and planet. I am very humbled and grateful," Potter said.

I'm sure you are, Tate thought mockingly.

Just then, Terry Peters walked in, followed by Carl Tubbs. Tubbs was a council elder with a passion for remembering and educating the colony about Earth's history. A short man, Tubbs looked the part—his wire-rimmed reading glasses were either firmly in place on his nose or perched on his forehead. He had an elongated thin nose and narrow, almost beady, eyes. His skin was snow white, as was the hair on his head and he was bone thin from head to toe. His voice was soft but confident and though frail to look at, the man had an erect posture and firm jaw.

As was his passion, Tubbs preached to the masses about man's greed and the eventual destruction of their planet. His life's goal was to remind the colony they had to live as a family and to always appreciate each other. Tubbs was a perfect emissary for the meeting.

And then there was Potter. Few men in the entire colony weighed more than what their body was designed for. There wasn't enough food to go around to allow someone to get fat. Yet Potter always seemed to carry twenty to thirty more pounds on his frame than anyone else. There was often talk that the man was secretly hoarding food, but no one ever confronted him about it.

Balding, with a brash comb-over, Potter was broad-shouldered barrel-chested with thick bulging arms. From the waist up, he was an imposing figure. But the man's legs reminded one of a Sandhill Crane's as the boney appendages were stick-thin. Tate often wondered how they held him erect as the laws of gravity would seem to make them impossible to carry his top-heavy form.

"Are we ready to go?" John Jacob's said.

"Where are ya goin' with that, John?" Terry Peters asked as he stared at the rifle slung over Jacob's shoulder.

"We can't travel that distance without weapons. Even though there hasn't been a scavenger sightin' anywhere near the rendezvous point, there is still the possibility," Jacobs said firmly, "Look at what just happened."

With a stunned look, Peters pleaded with his leader, "Lawrence? Please. We can't take a weapon with us. What will these space travelers think if'n they see us armed?"

"I understand yar concern Terry, but John is right. We must be prepared just in case. So, when we get close, and we know that everythin' is on the up and up, I will have John secure the weapon in a safe hidin' spot," Tate said.

"But—"

"Sorry, Terry. But we cain't take any chances. Now, let's head out, or we'll be late."

Chapter 14

"This is the Captain. We are now entering Earth's atmosphere. Our rendezvous point is an area just on the outskirts of what was known as the Rocky Mountains situated within Colorado, USA. There is a clearing at the provided coordinates that will allow us sufficient room to land and to set up a base camp as needed. Once on the ground, we will test the atmosphere for contaminants that couldn't be detected from space. We will also fortify the area from any native wildlife utilizing the boundary shielding system. After we are sure that there is nothing that can harm us, we will send out the perimeter set-up teams.

"On a personal note, I don't know how the rest of you feel about these recent developments, but to be the first Martians to set foot on our species' home planet—well, for me there are no words. So, hang on and buckle up, cause here we go. Captain out," Flynn said as he tapped off his com-link. "Mr. Cummings, bring us in."

Once on the ground, the crew went about their designated duties securing their ship and setting up their workstations for all the tasks soon at hand. Flynn sat in his chair reviewing multiple reports about Earth's atmosphere, climate conditions, and local terrain. The results from the testing seemed relatively normal. But something from the atmospheric test results had him puzzled. He'd been trying to come to terms with what he was looking at but couldn't figure it out, and it bugged him.

"Captain?" Chief of Security Belinda Grant called out.

"Yes, Lieutenant?" Flynn responded, though he didn't lift his head from what he was reading.

"Something odd. I see two groups outside our perimeter. One has five in its party, and there are thirty-seven, no thirty-eight in the other group," Grant said with surprise clearly in her voice.

"Show me," Flynn said as he powered down his data system and moved to her side.

"Here, this is the group of five," Grant indicated as she tapped a few icons on one of her screens. Five heat-identified life forms walked along a trail that led toward the clearing and ship. "These men are no more than 150 meters away from our position. The other faction is spread out behind the first group in an arc. They are probably another 200 or so meters back."

Flynn pondered the situation for a moment. He considered two possibilities. The group of five could be an advance party, with potentially armed reinforcements from their own camp behind them. This option was a concern as it would be a signal the group had ulterior motives for meeting them. The other theory was that a larger possibly hostile group to the five was following them. Flynn acted immediately as neither possibility was good. "Signal yellow alert and have the perimeter crew initiate security protocols for a possible incursion. Is the boundary barrier system up and running?"

"Yes sir," Grant stated firmly. There was now a definitive difference in her demeanor and attitude as the situation had ramped up the Lieutenant's focus.

"Send two drones out immediately. I want the first one over the five men. I want to see them and talk to them. Send the second drone above the other group but keep it 1 kilometer above them. Initiate the unit's stealth modes as I don't want either party to know the units are there...not until I decide the time is right."

Grant placed a small apparatus over her head. It had a sensor on one side that sat right above her left ear and a movable clear wand that slid across her right eye. This device allowed her to control the drones through thought without physically manipulating them with a tool.

Grant then slid her hand across the second screen on her console, tapped an icon that indicated drone number one, and typed in several commands. She did the same with drone number two. Within seconds, a 3-D image appeared above the Virtual Status Imagery System in front of the Captain's chair. The image showed a scaled version of the ship and a topographical depiction of the area around their landing spot.

Simultaneously to Grant's initiation, two portals opened on the rear of the M-453/E, and two drones the size of large platters sped out. Powered by magnetic impulse thrusting systems, these drones traveled in total silence, and, while in stealth mode, invisible.

The Captain followed the blue dots on the 3-D imagery movements of the drones. Once they left the surrounding of the ship's hull, the M-453/E's image disappeared, and then two new high-definition 3-D images came into focus. As the drones arrived at the ship's security perimeter, a crease appeared in the electronic containment spectrum just large enough for the speeding units to pass through. Once they cleared the shield the spectrum sealed.

Drone number one skimmed above the ground about thirty feet, sending back crystal-clear pictures of the terrain around the ship. Though the drones were controlled by the user's mental instructions, they were also equipped with AI sensory programmers that allowed them to speed through obstacles without fear of impact. With drone number one, it bobbed and weaved its way through the dense quadrant of trees without touching so much as a leaf.

Less than two minutes after leaving the ship, drone number one reached its destination. Thirty seconds later, drone number two did the same.

****

"How much more'n we gotta go," Potter asked Larry Jacobs.

"Bout' half a mile, I'd say," Jacobs answered.

"Christ! Couldn't we have foun'a place a little closer to home?" Potter complained in a choppy labored breath.

"Their Captain said they needed a large area to land, so we picked Buford's Bluff," Jacobs answered.

"Of course, I understand, and it makes perfect sense. But to be this far from our home, ya know, feels a bit risky. That's all I'm'a sayin'."

Yeah, sure. What you're really saying is that you're a fat bastard and so out of shape that the walk is killing you, Terry Peters thought to himself.

As they traveled the final distance, the team from Boulderside moved with purpose and a pointed wariness. The recent scavenger attack had taken the entire populace by surprise, and every swaying branch or windblown bush along the way looked sinister and foreboding.

Since the colony's move, no scavengers had been spotted within forty miles of the encampment. The biggest deterrent, the weather, had kept the flesh eaters from climbing higher—they couldn't cope with the colder climate. But now, with the nearby attack, all bets were off.

Trudging along in eerie silence, Tate rounded a corner of the trail and saw stand of shrubs, no more than thirty yards ahead, shake and quiver. Sounds of grunting and snorting came from the mass of wiry plants. Tate reactively threw up his hand to stop the group.

"What is it? What do ya see?" Potter blurted, almost tripping over Tate.

Tate grabbed Potter by the arm and ushered him back. He then motioned for Jacobs to move to the front of the pack.

"What it is Larry," Jacobs said in a tight whisper.

"There, about thirty yards up. Something just shook the hell out of those shrubs," Tate said as he pointed down the trail.

Jacobs slid by his team with gun raised shoulder height; ready to fend off a possible attack. The others huddled behind the man. Terry Peters, at the rear, raised his machete. At that moment, a squealing screech, loud and full of panic, came from the shrub. The bushes shook wildly, and then a family of wild boar came bursting out of the undergrowth straight down the path toward the men.

The four-unit family of pigs shrieked in annoyance as they galloped straight through the group. The colonists jostled and jumped out of the way as the unrepentant animals sprinted by without a glance back and disappeared down the trail. Though they were admittedly shaken, the five men laughed at the absurdity of the odd occurrence.

"Should'a shot 'em for food, nothin' like wild boar," Potter said.

"Yeah, ya say that now, but I'll bet ya a ham sandwich from that thin' that ya almost pissed your pants as they came a'racing toward us," Jacobs remarked. Everyone laughed again. As they regained what humility they had from the moment, the self-appointed representatives of the 650 residents of Boulderside set off again. Once they realized they were only a short distance away from the rendezvous site, their excitement mounted, though they weren't sure what to expect.

Behind them, a twig snapped . . .

"What was that?" Peters said as he froze in place.

"Not sure," Tate said as he glanced over his shoulder.

"Could be the boar?" Potter offered.

"No, those thin's are long gone. I'm thinkin' we better pick up the pace," Tate emphasized. As he turned back toward where he hoped the newcomer's ship was, a blue metallic sphere materialized directly in his path.

From the center of the sphere, a hologram image of Captain Everett appeared, "Hello gentlemen, this is Captain Everett. Which of you is Mr. Tate?"

Tate jumped back almost knocking the elderly Peters to the ground. "Christ, ya almost gave me a heart attack," Tate said as he regained his composure. "Yes, I am Larry Tate."

"Mr. Tate, I hesitate to presume, so I am going to come right out and ask. Our sensors have identified thirty-eight individuals behind you. Did you bring them? I see that one of your men is armed, are those behind you as well?"

Everyone in Tate's group spun around to look behind them. "Where–where are they? What do they look like? Can ya see 'em, how are they movin'? Are they a'comin' toward us?" Tate pleaded.

"I have sent a second drone to investigate these beings. It is arriving at their location now. When we first spotted them, the entire group ranged some 200 or so meters behind you. Six have now advanced and are only thirty or so meters to your left. Who are they, Mr. Tate?"

Tate moved directly in front of Flynn's image and spoke, "Captain, I promise ya, our group—the five standin' here—are the only ones that came from Boulderside. If'n there are others, they are not with us, and they are most likely dangerous. Very dangerous. Can ya help us? We cain't defend ourselves against that many. If'n they are hostiles, which I believe they must be, we are grossly outnumbered."

"Continue on your current heading Mr. Tate. Move quickly but stop as soon as you get to the clearing's edge and see our ship. Do not try to go any further. In the meantime, we will see who your pursuers are. This drone will stay on the path where it is now. If anyone or anything gets too close to you, we will know it. Captain out.

"Ms. Grant, do you have a visual on the second group?" Flynn asked as he swiveled his seat in her direction.

The drone is arriving at their position now. Visual identification in three, two, one . . ."

Chapter 15

Gary Sanchez, now healed and in solitary confinement, bolted up from his bed as the yellow alert signal echoed throughout the ship. He dashed to the door and banged on it. After no response, he turned to his room communication device next to the door. "What's going on? Let me out of here. I demand to see the Captain," he shouted into the unit.

A few seconds went by and then a calm and composed voice said, "Sir, I do not know the source of the emergency. But even if I did, I cannot let you out. You know that, so please stop banging on the door," Ensign Eric Stone said from a control room at the end of the corridor of the crew's quarters.

"Stony, you know I'm not a threat. For God's sake, we've been playing Triple Level Chess Trials almost every day since I got out of sick bay. At least come down to my room and show me what's happening on your wrist monitor. Please, I'm going crazy in here," Sanchez said in desperation.

The detainee put his ear to his door and listened, but he sensed no indication of movement by the ensign. Sanchez tapped the communicator again, "Come on, Stony, I promise I won't cause you any problems. I just want to see what's happening."

Several more seconds went by with nothing, no response, and no footfalls coming down the hall. Just as he was about to bang on the door again, Sanchez heard a noise. To the right of the door was a cane he'd used while recuperating from his leg injury. Sanchez snatched it up and moved to the opposite side of the door.

"You know, I shouldn't be doing this, especially since you haven't let me win a single game of TLCT. But I'm just as curious as you are, so I'm coming in," Eric Stone said. The Ensign tapped a code into an outside panel next to the detainee's door and waited. There was an electronic click, and then the door slid open. As it did, the Ensign lowered his head and tapped his wrist-monitor to get the latest on the events around the ship. "Not sure what we're going to get, but we ca…"

The cane came down on the back of the ensign's head knocking him to the ground and out cold.

"Sorry my friend, but I didn't come all this way not to see what's on this planet," Sanchez said as he began removing items from his unconscious victim. After he finished stripping the man of his wrist-monitor, com-link, and his Update-Linking-Portal, Sanchez gagged the ensign and then tied his hands and feet with his bed linens before dragging him into the closet. After closing the closet door, he grabbed food supplies and a few other odds and ends and stuffed them into a linen bag.

Sanchez went to the door and listened intently. When he heard nothing, he tapped the door activator and watched as the panel slid open. The stowaway glanced down the hall and saw no one. He shuffled out and crept down the corridor. He knew exactly where he was going—the quickest way out without being seen was the same way he got in—the loading dock bay.

Moving with purpose, Sanchez headed to the bottom of Lift Station number four, near the engine room's crew's quarters. The rest of the staff would be at their stations during the Yellow Alert, so this area should be clear. Just then, a power station diagnostics crewman sped by. He glanced at Sanchez, their eyes met, but the crewman didn't slow.

****

"Captain, are you seeing what I'm seeing?" Lieutenant Grant said.

"Yes," Everett responded as he studied the man. After a moment he said, "Is there something wrong with him? Is he inebriated? And why is he dressed or, should I say, undressed like that?" Flynn had asked the questions but knew his Security Officer was as clueless as he was. "Send the drone down and let's have a chat."

Grant mentally maneuvered the small disk-shaped unit above the bobbing man. "Disengaging stealth mode," Grant said as she tapped her screen.

"This is Captain Flynn Everett of the Martian M-453/E spaceship. May I have a word with you?" Flynn asked. The man's face was blotchy with patches of raw blemished skin. Open wounds on his arms and chest oozed something resembling a mixture of blood and pus. His scalp had large patches of hair missing with gnarly webbings of flesh sticking up in spikes or laying over in flaps. It looked like he had been in a fight with a rabid animal. As the drone hovered almost six feet off the ground, the man stared at the craft with vacant eyes.

"Can you hear me?" Flynn asked.

The man continued to gaze inanely without answering. He only swayed and rocked like he was on the deck of a ship in an ocean storm. Suddenly, his right arm, which had been hanging slack at his side, swung at the drone. It was a slow and cumbersome movement.

The drone, with over 1,000 sensors in its navigational system, easily pulled back and away. The man tried again, this time with the other arm. This attempt delivered the same result. The swaying man then swung both arms at the blue orb going at it in a mindless effort of flailing limbs.

From the bushes came two more men, both in a similarly disheveled condition. And then two more. The five gaped at the drone in apparent inquisitiveness, but no one spoke. The first man continued his mindless attempts to grab at the drone. And, though it was more than obvious that he would never reach it, the other four men joined him in the same absurd attempts to capture the unit.

"Target each and send a message Ms. Grant," Flynn said. The Lieutenant tapped her screen a few times and then looked at her Captain, nodded that she was ready, and then tapped the screen once more. A brilliant blue streak shot from the drone five times. The laser-like beams struck each man directly in the sternum knocking each to the ground. The Lieutenant had set the drone's attack so it wouldn't kill; just stun the beings.

As the scavengers lay motionless, an ear-shattering shriek came from behind the drone. The unit's visual lens instantly swiveled towards the sound. Standing maybe ten feet away was another man. He was taller than the others and carried himself with a stiffer back and more erect posture. He also appeared healthier with no open wounds or blotchy skin. He was pointing at the drone and screaming, no screeching.

****

Tate and his men made it to the clearing's edge and then stopped dead in their tracks. The five stood awestruck as they stared at the gleaming spacecraft in the middle of the field. It was easily 200-meters wide and 300 or so meters long and reminded the Boulderside's leader of pictures that he'd seen in science fiction books—a massive hulking craft easily eight to ten stories high.

It was shaped like an early century stealth bomber, with thick multi-story wings on either side of tall center structure. The craft had three enormous exhaust ports in the back, with the center port two times the size of the ones on either side. A large round section in the front of the ship looked to be the bridge with a broad viewing screen across the front.

The spacecraft was held above the ground by four massive claw-like legs extending down from the hull. Each limb contained three hydraulic stabilizing bars. These rods connected at the bottom to round feet, which protruded out and then down onto the turf. The entire craft was stunning.

"I don't see anyone, do ya?" Peters asked the other four.

"No. No, I don't. What should we do?" Jacobs asked Tate. "Hey, wait a minute. Over there, comin' out of the back of the ship. That must be one of the crew. Why's he a'runnin' in the opposite direction?"

"Not gettin' a good feelin' guys," Potter said under his breath. "Where's he a'goin?"

The five men watched as the fleeing man ran straight towards the woods beyond the clearing's edge. Just before he entered the tree line, he stopped and tapped something on his wrist. Suddenly, the air in front of the man began to quiver and glimmer. It was a momentary blur, something like a 20th century carnival mirror.

They watched as the man looked around, stepped through the blur, and disappeared into the woods.

"Well, that was curious," Tate said.

"Yeah, and was it just me or did that guy look like a giant?" Potter said as he stared at the spot the large man just disappeared into.

"Mr. Tate," Flynn's voice called from the drone.

"Yes, Captain," Tate responded.

"I'm a bit confused as to what is happening and would like an explanation. The men I just tried to communicate with, what's wrong with them?"

Tate looked at everyone in his group. His shoulders rose and then fell in resignation. He turned back to the drone and was about to confess when a shriek that could rival any from a classic horror movie pierced the air. Tate's group seemed to shrink back in shock, moving as one, back and away from the sound.

"Stop. Do not come any closer toward the ship. We have a highly energized perimeter shield a few feet from where you stand. It won't kill you if you lightly encounter it, but you'll know you did, I can assure you."

"Captain, please, let us in. These bein's, they. . . they are cannibals. They will kill us and eat us if'n ya don't let us in," Potter cried out.

Flynn looked around the bridge, "Did I just hear that right?"

There was silence for several seconds, enough time for the foliage to explode with bodies as one after another of the second group of beings closed in on Tate's men.

"Please—I will tell ya everythin', just do not let these creatures touch us. If'n they do, we are finished," Tate pleaded. At that moment, a quivering wave of energy appeared in front of where the colonists stood. They were too far away to clearly see what occurred when the man they watched earlier crossed through the pulsating field behind the ship. But now, the energy shield was unmistakably visible as a static-lined opening separated wide enough for the five men to cross.

"Step through, quickly," Flynn instructed. The men did so just as another high-pitched squeal rang out behind them. As if the animalistic screech was a signal for an attack, two-dozen more beings came crashing out of the tree line and bushes that encircled the clearing.

Once Tate and his group ran past the energy field's opening, the hole in the quivering shield closed with a buzzing *SNAP*. Frank Potter, stork legs straining to keep up with his terror, was unconvinced the shield could really protect them. He jerked his head around to see how close the scavengers were, lost his balance, tripped, and fell face-first into the grass-covered earth.

Though the dreaded horde moved slowly and cumbersome when at a walking pace, they were surprisingly fast when a food source appeared. With teeth chomping wildly, one of the ravenous beings saw a fallen prey and raced at Potter. He dove headfirst for the man with reckless flesh-devouring abandon.

The first of his body parts to hit the starship's protective energy shield was the scavenger's face, chin out, and teeth wildly gnawing. When it did, there was a loud bang, like that of a power transformer exploding, but with no sparks. The hurtling being's forward momentum and the repellent force of the shield ricocheted its body like a fastball being flushed by a well-muscled batter.

When the pummeled body crashed to the ground, some ten or so meter's away, its head was split open like a cleaved melon. Before the rest of the screaming horde understood that something was wrong, five more lay dead on the ground around him.

The human flesh eaters weren't totally mindless inept beings, though you couldn't call them very bright either. But they eventually became aware enough to know that charging after Tate's group into the clearing was no longer a good idea. For several moments the throng just stood around and gaped as the five colonists made their way toward the ramp of the ship's cargo bay. The huge ship itself seemed to go unnoticed.

Everett's voice came from the drone, which had come back inside the shield and made its way to the Earthlings. "Gentlemen, go to the ramp and walk to the top. To your left, you will see a large glass enclosure. Enter it. Do not be concerned; it is merely a decontamination chamber. A fine mist will envelop you and rid you of any potentially harmful contaminants before you enter our ship. A red light will illuminate the room after you enter, and the door will seal. When the light turns green, the second door on the opposite side will open. Walk through that door and into the room on the other side. My Science Officer, Lieutenant Commander Canfield, will be there to meet you. She will take you to a conference room. I will arrive shortly after that."

Though somewhat hesitant the five men did as instructed and moved up the ramp to the glass chamber. The area inside was easily fifteen meters square and appeared to be large enough to accommodate at least ten men. As the door closed behind them, they heard a vacuum sound. Seconds later, a red light came on, and a light gray mist shot from nozzles on the ceiling and from small apertures throughout the floor and walls.

The vapor rushed into and around every crack, crevice, and orifice of their bodies. It was almost as if the microscopic particles were living entities as the mist seemed to search their forms for entry points. The sensation of the mist going into their ears, eyes and nose was unsettling. No one talked, but each seemed taken aback by the intrusion.

After a few minutes of this swirling haze, the red light flashed followed by another vacuum sound. A large vent in a sidewall of the chamber extracted the mist. Another swooshing sound caused the men's ears to pop, and then a green light flashed above the opposite door. Tate opened the door and followed a corridor to another entrance where he came face to chest with Melanie Ann Canfield—all perfectly proportioned seven-foot-one-inch of her.

Chapter 16

Flynn sat in the bridge and watched the lurking throng still hovering around the ship's defensive shield. The beings continued to test the obstinacy of the unseen force preventing them from venturing any closer to his ship.

Occasionally, one of them would reach out with a finger or two until the vibration of the electronic pulses let them know they were about to get zapped. The being would pull back only to have another do the same thing. And then, one of them would seem to lose patience and would race down the path and hurl his body into the perimeter defense's clutches, only to be catapulted back through the air and onto the ground in a pile. When they landed, they were severely injured or dead.

The captain was jerked out of his trance of these constant illogical actions by a hail on his com-link. "Captain?"

"This is Everett."

"The colony's emissaries have successfully completed the decontamination process and are in the level three conference center," Melanie Canfield reported.

"I'm on my way."

"One thing," Melanie added hesitantly.

"And that would be?"

"Well, they are a bit shell-shocked by us. To give you an idea, I am a good foot or so taller than the tallest of them, and you, well, you are going to be a virtual giant to them."

"Hmm...You know that fact may not be a bad thing," Flynn offered and then tapped off his com link. "Commander Parks, you have the bridge," he said as he left the room.

Flynn headed toward the bridge's lift station door but stopped short of getting on. Turning towards the images still being projected by the 3-D console, he said, "Lieutenant Grant, please let me know if circumstances change in any way with those beings. If they move away, send a drone to follow them. If they try other means to find egress past our shield, I want to know."

"Aye, aye, Captain," Grant replied.

Everett made his way to the level-three conference room. Two crewmen from the ship's security team stood on either side of the conference room door. They stiffened to attention as their captain strode past and into the chamber. Seated around the table were the five men from Boulderside, as well as Lieutenant Commander Canfield, Commander Brad Cummings, and ship's Doctor Leonard Carlson. When Everett entered, everyone stood.

Flynn, towering above his guests, said in a commanding trombone voice, "Gentlemen, welcome to our ship. My name is Captain Flynn Everett. You've met Commander Cummings, Lieutenant Commander Canfield, and Doctor Carlson. I trust they have seen to your needs since coming aboard," Flynn said matter of fact.

The men nodded in agreement.

"Good. To begin with, let me assure you that everyone onboard this ship is overjoyed with having found you. However, I must admit, I am torn with conflict. What should be occurring is an exchange of dialogue filled with the excitement of our discovery of each other. This discussion will occur, I'm sure. Yet, as Captain of this ship, I must make sure that the welfare and safety of my crew is always my priority. So, our first order of business is the situation with those others outside at this moment."

"Captain Flynn," Tate said as he leaned forward. "Thank ya for seein' us and for yar hospitality. Believe me, I understand yar concern and I will try to explain," Tate said.

After a brief hesitation, Tate began, "Our books and documents reference how in 2057, WW III broke out. Unlike the previous two world wars that was concentrated in Europe and Asia, this one was a global conflict that wreaked havoc across the entire globe.

The United States, which hadn't had an enemy attack on its home soil in over two centuries, was not only bombed, but was hit with nuclear weapons. Durin' one of the assaults a secret facility that harbored the world's deadliest diseases and pathogens was compromised. Captain, that is when the real war began."

Tate's eyes closed and he shook his head in solemn reflection as he mentally recalled reading about the horrors of the conflict. "The unleashin' of this conglomeration of highly toxic compounds along with the radioactivity of the nuclear warheads ended up causin' a biomolecular alteration in many of the survivin' humans. What ya witnessed outside is the evolutionary results of that alteration. I'm sure ya have read fiction stories about zombies. Well, these bein's are real, and they are far worse than zombies."

"You are joking of course," Doctor Carlson remarked. "I mean, it is scientifically impossible for a zombie to be real. Dead bodies cannot walk. Their nervous system would not be active; they would be unable to move any of their body parts. They couldn't see or smell, and the eating of other humans, impossible. Their digestive system wouldn't be functioning, which means that even if they could bite and chew, anything they consumed, dead or alive, would eventually back up and fill their gullet, throat, and mouth. And those are just the immediate reasons that jump out of my mind. I'm sure there are many, many others."

"Yes Doctor, yar theories are accurate," Tate replied. "The problem is that these bein's are not dead. Documents offer little, but what they do say is that the new and altered pathogens wormed their way into susceptible human hosts and changed them.

"The obvious issue, and the one that is the most appallin', is that these bein's thrive on eatin' live flesh. They eat any livin' creature they capture; however, humans have become their food of choice as they are easier for them to catch than wild animals. Because of that, these horrid creatures ya see outside have hunted the planet's non-infected people as their sustenance for years. And, because we didn't have the appropriate means to stop them, we believe they now outnumber the non-affected.

"If'n ya were not killed and eaten when attacked and bitten, and the blood or saliva from an infected came in contact with any orifice or opening in yar body—yar eyes, ears, mouth, or an open wound, ya became infected and would quickly turn. One other glarin' thin', and it is truly the ultimate in our possible and eventual demise. These devils breed."

"My God," Brad Cummings mouthed. The astonishment on his face was intense.

"Yes," Frank Potter agreed. "And though they can and do breed like rabbits, only a small percentage of our women can bear children, and we have no idea why. So, while their species, if'n ya can call them that, grow and multiply, our colonies either stay somewhat stagnant in size, or we wither away and die."

Tate chimed back in, "Captain, I'm afraid that the Earth that yar ancestors left is a very different one than the Earth we try to survive in today. I am sorry we didn't explain this in our earlier communications, but we need yar help. And to be perfectly blunt, I believed that the only way ya would do so was to meet us in person and see that we are good and decent people."

Flynn was momentarily speechless. He looked around the table in subtle but sincere shock. When his ship arrived in Earth's atmosphere and contacted Tate's group, he'd felt elated. But with this revelation—he felt somewhat paralyzed. To believe that the planet supported a group of living human flesh-eating beings seemed beyond his worst fears. He cleared his throat and was about to reply when he was interrupted by his com-link.

"Captain Flynn?"

Flynn tapped the communication device. "Yes, Ms. Grant. Has there been a change outside?"

"No, Captain," Grant said. "The group continues to display their odd behavior. They seem somewhat mindless and are showing no additional signs of aggression."

Flynn looked at Tate with his brow furrowing slightly. "Yes, I understand. So, if things are the same with them, is there something else?"

"Oh, yes sir, sorry. It's Mr. Sanchez. He's missing."

Chapter 17

Flynn stared at Melanie with a look of utter frustration and shook his head. Gary Sanchez had now pushed him past any sort of tolerance he might have offered the stowaway.

"I will meet security in his room in ten minutes. Flynn out." The captain turned to his guests. "Gentlemen, to say that I am a little shocked by what you have related here today, well, I guess that would be the understatement of the century. I know we have much more to discuss, but, unfortunately, I have another problem that must be addressed at once. Commander Cummings will take you to our dining hall for some food and beverages. If you will indulge me, let's meet back here in one hour. Agreed?"

"Of course, Captain," Tate said as Flynn stood. "But can I ask one question before ya go?"

"Yes, Mr. Tate."

"Are all of yar people as big and tall as ya four? I mean, look at us. We are average sized for Earthlings. And since ya came from Earth, how did ya become so big?"

Flynn chuckled and turned to Doctor Carlson. "Doc, you want to handle this one?"

Carlson straightened in satisfaction and stood. "By all means, Captain, it would be my pleasure. "Mr. Tate, though I haven't thoroughly analyzed the causes, as I am sure there are several, I believe the most glaring reason would be the difference in gravity between

Mars and Earth. Even with our Gravitational Balance System, which we use to simulate Earth's gravity, there is still enough of a variance that appears to have caused our bodies to evolve. We have adapted to our environment as so many species do. In fact, because of this growth, the entire crew has had to take ongoing supplemental injections to compensate for the denser gravity here on Earth."

"Yes, and they are bit unsettling, to say the least," Brad Cummings said.

"Well, whatever the reasons, your size is goin' to cause a bit of a commotion with the people here," Jacobs said as the rest of the group around the table stood.

****

Flynn and Melanie headed toward Sanchez's room when an announcement came over the ship's intercom system. "Doctor Carlson, please come to the deck three crewmen quarters, unit twelve."

"Sanchez's room. It figures," Flynn said as the two began to run. After taking the lift down to the appropriate level, the two exited to see crewman Eric Stone being helped out of Sanchez's room.

"Stony, are you ok?" Flynn asked the shaken crewman.

"Yes sir, just a bit woozy. He hit me with something as I came in. I should have known better sir. I'm sorry," Eric Stone said as he shuffled to a seat at his security station.

"Yes, well, there will be time to discuss that. I'm sure Mr. Towers and Ms. Grant will have plenty to say about it when you make your report," Flynn said, though he had a hint of humor in his voice.

"Yes sir, I'm sure they will." Crewman Stone related what had happened right up to the moment he was knocked unconscious.

"So, no idea where he might have gone?" Flynn queried.

"Sorry, no sir," Stone said. "He was so eager to find out what was happening outside, so maybe?"

Doctor Carlson entered the room, went straight to Crewman Stone's side, and physically examined the knot on the back of his head. He then removed an analyzer scanner, tapped in some info, and released it above Stone's head. As it floated there a broad beam swept down the back of Stone's head, and halfway down his spine. Once the electronic examination ceased, Carlson grabbed the scanner and checked the results.

"You'll live," Carlson said. "No concussion or fracture, but that knot's not going away anytime soon. I'll give you something for the pain–though I fear I have nothing for the pain you'll be receiving from your superiors."

Eric Stone looked at the Captain who then looked at Doctor Carlson. "Oh, already gone down that road, have we? Well, let's get you to sick bay and have a closer look, just in case. Can you walk on your own?" Carlson asked.

"Yes sir," Stone replied, wobbling as he stood.

Doctor Carlson grabbed the young crewman's arm and guided him toward the lift. As the two disappeared into the unit, Flynn's com-link signaled. "Flynn here," the captain said.

"Captain, Grant here. You wanted to know if anything changed outside? Well, it has. You better come to the bridge right away."

✷✷✷✷

As soon as the door opened to the bridge, Flynn demanded, "Ms. Grant?"

"Yes, sir. No changes for most of the time you were gone. The remaining beings that were neither dead nor injured continued to test the shield with pokes and prods, even as illogical as that sounds. And then, about ten minutes ago, this happened," Grant said as she tapped her screen. Instantly, a recorded image appeared showing Gary Sanchez emerging from the trees directly behind the creatures at the shield.

"Seeing this, I immediately sent a drone to warn Mr. Sanchez or to help him if he needed it. I believe he must have been returning to the ship when he stumbled on the bobbing and weaving horde. It looked like he was contemplating an introduction when he stopped, wisely so, and then made his way back to the trees where he took cover.

"The one we believe might be the leader began sniffing the air. A few seconds after that, he started screaming like a Martian banshee and took off in Mr. Sanchez's direction. The rest of the creatures raced after that guy with my drone following," Grant said.

"And where is Sanchez now?" Flynn said.

"I'm not sure. I eventually moved the drone up to the head of the pack and began sweeping the area thinking the drone's sensors might locate him. So far, it hasn't detected him, which is odd. I can only surmise that he is blocking our scans somehow."

"Ms. Grant, have a security party of four meet me at the rear disembarkation station. Make sure Commander Towers is with them.

Have them bring sidearms as well as laser rifles. Also, have Mr. Cummings meet me there. Keep looking for Mr. Sanchez and let me know if you find him."

"Yes sir," Grant said.

Once Flynn and Melanie got on the lift and the door closed, he turned to her and said, "If those creatures don't catch Sanchez and eat him, I'm going to kill him myself."

Chapter 18

Gary Sanchez heard the scream. The noise did not seem human nor like any animal sound he'd ever known. Fear embraced him like a straitjacket, squeezing all restraint and reason out of his mind. The Martian didn't hesitate. Though he had no idea of where to go, he took off and ran as fast has he could down the trail heading in the opposite direction of the scream–and the spaceship.

Hanging branches and vines seemed to reach out and grab at him like an octopus grasping its prey with its tangling tentacles. He swatted them away with mad fury for about eighty yards, still running at top speed, when he turned a sharp corner and realized, too late, that the path abruptly vanished. He tried to stop, couldn't, and went headlong into a thick stand of dense brush.

The seven-and-a-half-foot man tried to stay on his feet but the ground beneath him had suddenly evaporated. Sanchez began somersaulting as he flew over a ledge and down a steep incline before bursting through a wall of bushes. Now completely out of control, he splatted on his back in a muddy drainage rut that went straight down. The washout twisted and turned like a toboggan run and spun him like a top.

The twisting Sanchez threw his hands and legs out groping for any purchase, but there was nothing but gooey slick mud that slipped through his fingers like soup. And now, instead of slowing down, he was picking up speed.

After traveling some twenty meters down the embankment, flailing and in full panic mode, the foliage around Sanchez disappeared exposing a vast spring-filled lake. The furrow he catapulted down ended about three meters above the water. The enormous man flew out of the rut and sailed through the air before landing at the water's edge with a muddy thwack.

He lay there for several seconds as he gathered his wits and tried to shake away the stars dancing around his head. At that moment, he heard loud grunts and groans from above. Fear once again electrified his already fractured nerves. He jumped up and looked for a way out. Other than a small waterfall on the far side, he only saw rain washout ruts.

After spending a few seconds focusing on the waterfall, Sanchez thought he saw an opening—a momentary flash–as the water separated for a brief second. It could be a possible place to hide. The problem was that the only way to get there was the lake. Swimming on Mars was unheard of.

The distance between the waterfall and where he stood might as well have been a thousand miles. Sanchez whined like a whimpering child who has lost sight of its parents. He decided to make his way up one of the other washout ruts.

Before he took his first step a scavenger came flying down the rut and hurled straight into Sanchez's chest. The Martian rocketed into the lake with the creature on top of him. As the two crashed into the water, something grabbed onto the Martian's arm. It felt like a sharp pinch. He looked down and saw the creature's head where he felt the pain. *Was the hideous thing biting him?*

Panicking, he pummeled his fist into the attacker's face, splitting its nose down the middle like a filleted fish, then shoved the now gasping creature toward the middle of the lake. As Sanchez floundered to get righted, he realized that the bottom swiftly slanted down toward the middle of the lake. He balanced himself, dug his feet in and began to walk.

Fearful of another attack, Sanchez slogged as fast as he could, desperate to reach the shore. He had to get out of the water and climb up the embankment before the thing flailing behind him righted itself and took up the pursuit. If he didn't make it out, he'd have to turn and stand his ground to fight. The thought made him sick to his already reeling stomach.

Sanchez chanced a glance over his shoulder to gauge the distance between where he was, and where the being had been. He was shocked to see that it hadn't advanced toward him at all. In fact, the thing was thrashing about in the water like a fish trying to throw off an angler's hook. Seconds later, the creature simply sank down and out of sight.

Sanchez wasn't sure if the strange being was walking along the bottom like he was, or not, but he was taking no chances. He doubled his efforts using his arms and legs to propel him out of the water. Just as he got to a point where the water was at his knees, another beast flew out of the shrubs, down the rut, and out into the water. And then another, and another.

The earthlings splashed in at about the same spot the first had gone. Sanchez assumed they would pop up any minute and swim after him, but other than a roiling of water, and an occasional exposed thrashing hand, no one came up.

Making his way to shore, Sanchez searched around and found a washout that was drier than the one he'd come down. He dug his heels into the sides and clambered the twenty or so meters up the bowl-shaped crevice. By the time he got to the top, he was gasping with fatigue.

Back on level ground, but with terror still driving him, he pushed through the thick clinging underbrush for several minutes until he found a trail. When he looked down, he saw large footprints, easily as large as his own. He placed his foot in one and realized it was made from his boot. He traced along the footsteps for about ten minutes until the off-ramp of the ship came into view.

In gleeful exuberance, Sanchez dashed up to the electronic defense shield and removed the personal access unit from his pocket. He tapped the access initiator; nothing happened. The shield held, and no opening appeared. He tapped it again, still nothing. He turned the unit over and examined it. The device had a crack along the back and seemed to have been tainted by a water incursion. "Great, that's just great!" Sanchez wailed as he slammed the useless contraption to the ground.

He inched toward the shield being careful not to get too close. If he made full contact it could singe his skin, or worse. He hoped that the ship's sensors would pick up his proximity and alert someone to come out and rescue him. He dared not shout for help, more of those things could be close by.

The hairs on Sanchez's arms, neck, and head began to move, lifting and swaying like reeds in a tidal pool, as the shields electronic channeling made peripheral contact. He took a step back and began waving his hands and jumping up and down–and that's when a scavenger burst onto the path behind him. He was less than thirty meters away. The two locked eyes, Sanchez's bright blue, but now filled with panic. The scavenger's, a bloodshot mire of greenish brown and red, filled with hunger.

The ravenous creature let out a shriek that cut straight into Sanchez, boring a hole into every nerve ending of his body. As the stowaway stared in shock at the hideous-looking man, a dozen more scavengers abruptly rushed into view. The group raced toward the terror-stricken man, their faces contorted with looks of maniacal rage and hunger lust. With lips peeled back, and rotting teeth exposed, the charging horde looked to Sanchez like a pack of rabid animals. To make the moment even more nerve-wracking was the rapid chomping chattering noise their teeth made.

The Martian glanced to his left and then to his right. He had to run, look for a means of escape. On his left, the dense tree line came up to the spot where he believed the shield stopped. Not enough room to go that way. To his right, a small path ran along the border of the shield. But if he took that path it would lead him back to the small clearing where he first saw the group of creatures.

If others were left in reserve, he would run straight into them. And though he was much larger, and could probably hold off four of five, there would be no way he could defend himself from the large gang now giving chase. Sanchez had no real choice. He ran to his right.

Most Martians were in tremendous physical shape, toned and muscular. Sanchez was lazy and gluttonous, rarely exercised, and had poor stamina. These traits normally would leave him sluggish, forcing him to stop often to catch his breath. But the adrenal fear racing through his body gave him amazing impetus. He used his long legs to eat up huge chunks of terrain. In mere seconds he had easily distanced himself from the voracious group. Once he got to the clearing those pursuing were just arriving at the spot he'd been standing when the first scavenger emerged on the trail.

Three of the creatures hadn't slowed for the turn and ran headlong into the shield. The electronic barrier violently repelled their advance, and they were hurtled backward. Two of the beings smashed into tree trunks and fell to the ground unmoving. The third flew headfirst into the underbrush. He lay in a crumpled mass with his legs protruding from the greenery. The grizzled limbs shook and jerked as if being jabbed with an electronic cattle prod. None of the fiend's companions paid any heed nor did they slow to check out the condition of their fallen comrades.

When Sanchez had at first dashed down the exit ramp of the ship and made his way through the shield, he had assumed that he would quickly find a town or city to explore. He would blend in and mingle with the citizens and see for himself what the current inhabitants were like. Maybe he would even meet their leaders and become the liaison for the Martian mission. But he had explored for thirty minutes, and his only discovery was a never-ending vista of trees, prickly vines, and unforgiving underbrush.

After climbing some thirty feet up a nubby pine Sanchez had looked in every direction and seen nothing but more trees. He hadn't conceived that he would find nothing.

As he was wandering through the countryside, he questioned *'Why had that idiot Everett landed in the middle of nowhere?'* And now, as he'd finally grasped the considerable disparity in size between him and the earth beings, he realized that he would have stuck out like a man amongst children. And why hadn't he taken Stone's com-link? He could be calling for help right now. But a com-link had a tracking device implanted in it, and they would have known where he was. Something he hadn't wanted to happen.

Sanchez lost all reservations and began shouting, hoping that someone would hear and come to his aid.

Another shriek!

This time the sound was in front of him. He came to a sliding stop. He anxiously glanced around and saw that his original pursuers were still fifty meters away. The shield was now at his back, thick foliage and underbrush lay in front of him, and to his right and left, more of those things. My God, he would have to make a stand and fight. He'd probably be captured, or worse. He swallowed hard and reactively curled his hands into fists.

In a desperate attempt to gain protection, Sanchez cowered back into the foliage using the dense plants as a rear barrier. He would then use the ship's forcefield as a weapon. When they came at him, he would use his size and strength advantage to shove them into the electronic wall. It may not kill them, but it might stun them and possibly knock them out of the altercation.

A pack of around ten flesh-eating fiends closed in.

Sweat poured down Sanchez's terror-stricken face, and his adrenalin had his nervous system screaming. His breath was coming in gasps. He thought he might black out at any moment. When the first attacker was no more the ten feet away, the much bigger man shrank back even further as he noticed his foe's features.

The shirtless being's skin appeared ravaged, with large blotchy sores and welts along his cheeks and down his neck and torso. He was human, he guessed—no doubt emaciated with some ungodly Earth-borne disease. The thing's eyes were sunken deep into the skull, and one side of its nose was almost rotted away.

Then, like an animal about to attack its prey, his assailant's lips curled back showing a row of decayed jagged teeth and gums burnt red with infection. Growling like a rabid savage, with foaming saliva dripping down its face, the earthling began chomping its teeth up and down with a hideous clacking sound.

Chapter 19

"I have him," Security officer Grant said over the communicator.

"Go," Flynn responded.

"He's to your left, seventy-five meters. He's about to be overtaken by several of the creatures. I sent the drone to intercept."

"I see them. Alert Mr. Sanchez to stay in place until we arrive to guard his re-entry through the shield," Flynn instructed.

"Aye, Aye, Captain."

****

Sanchez looked for a weapon, anything that could keep the beasts at bay. He rummaged through the brush in search of a stick or branch, anything to stab or club them. He found nothing. The bushes scraped and tore at his hands and arms as he frantically searched through the undergrowth. He could hear the grunting, snarling beasts closing in from both directions. The festering things crashed through the brush with reckless abandon. An uncontrolled scream of fatalistic terror burst from Sanchez's mouth, and with this exhaled screech so went his fighting spirit.

Shrinking back and down, Sanchez closed his eyes, waiting for the inevitable. Then, the unmistakable sounds of a stunning laser blast jerked him out of his stupor. He searched around with a renewed look of hope, and, as he did, a scavenger leaped at him from the trail. Though the much bigger man could have easily subdued this lone aggressor, Sanchez instead cowered back and once again closed his eyes in defeat.

As the scavenger flew, now only a couple of feet from landing on top of the cringing Sanchez, a laser blast hit the form mid-flight. This time, unlike earlier, the laser beam seemed more powerful, with a darker blue streak that slammed into the hurtling figure. The shot pummeled the attacker's body splitting it almost in two and causing it to fly into the shrubs where it vanished among the foliage.

Expecting but not receiving the attack, Sanchez rose, tears streaming down his face, and watched as one of the ship's drones positioned itself in front of him. The small sphere held the rest of the attackers at bay spinning back and forth as it sent intense beams of brilliant light at his aggressors.

"Mr. Sanchez stay where you are. A security team is on the way," an electronic voice said from the drone.

Sanchez turned to see Flynn running at his position with several others close behind. They were armed with laser pistols and rifles. "Oh, thank God," Sanchez screamed in jubilation as he made his way in their direction.

"This way, and hurry," Flynn said as he tapped his com-link once. "Ms. Grant, if you will kindly provide an entry for Mr. Sanchez."

A shivering crease appeared in the shield a few meters away. Sanchez dashed through, eyes bulging wild with panicked elation. He raced past his saviors not stopping, his legs and arms flying in all directions.

"Sanchez, stop!" Flynn yelled. But the terrified man only ran faster. Flynn grabbed a rifle from Brad Cummings and aimed at the fleeing man.

"Captain?" Cummings said hesitantly.

"Don't worry, I'm not going to kill him," Flynn said with reservation in his voice, "Well, maybe a little…"

"SANCHEZ!" Flynn yelled, and then he sent a quick laser burst that hit the ground right in front of the sprinting stowaway. The shot hit the turf and threw up a cloud of dirt and debris causing Sanchez to slide to a stop with his hands in the air. He was only a few meters from the ramp and safety, but he stayed in place, legs now unable to move on their own.

"Mr. Towers please take two of your men and see to it that our friend goes through decontamination, and then securely lock him in his room–and I mean securely. Use chains and shackles if you must. Oh, and make sure he has no weapons of any kind in his room or upon his body. Strip him naked if need be."

Towers and two others sped off toward Sanchez. As the four men disappeared into the ship, Flynn turned his attention back to the lurking scavengers just outside of the shield. As he walked up to the mob of creatures, now less than twenty-five in number—several had been rendered unconscious or dead—one of the beings at the perimeter raced at him.

His movements were jerky and ape-like as he plunged headfirst into the ship's energy field. Once again, the beast was catapulted backwards and to the ground. The one who appeared to be the leader let out a few grunting noises while gesturing back with his hands. These obtuse instructions had the rest of his pack moving backward a step or two.

Flynn strode confidently toward that man, stopping only a couple of feet from the invisible barrier that separated the two factions. The disheveled man, seemingly just as curious, walked toward Flynn. The two men regarded each other for several silent moments. Flynn finally broke the moment as he asked in English, "Can you speak?"

The man opposite of Everett, moving ever so slightly from side to side, said nothing. Every now and then, he would raise his eyes to meet Everett's for a second or two, before lowering his gaze to the ground. Everett spoke in French, and then Italian. Each time, he received the same silence and random stares. Flynn tried a few other languages, including Russian and Chinese. Martians had kept many of Earth's languages alive on Mars with the hope of someday having the chance to use them on a return visit. But the creature never responded to any of the languages and showed little or no hint of recognition.

Flynn gave up and turned to leave. As he did, the man grunted and stomped his feet, seemingly in protest to Flynn's non-permissioned departure. Everett turned and regarded the man once more. This time, his adversary lifted his head slightly and kept it there. Flynn believed this to be a positive cognizant action.

"Shall we try this again? Can you communicate?" Once again, nothing. Then the creature lifted its eyes and stared straight at Flynn. He tilted his head ever so little to one side, and then the next. "You do understand, at least a little?" At this, it appeared that one of the corners of the creature's mouth rose slightly. And then it turned and grunted like a trained seal before sprinted away with his followers close at hand.

"Interesting," Flynn said under his breath.

"Did you see?" Cummings asked. "He responded—sort of."

"Yes," Flynn said with a nod. "There is something there. The rest of his group seemed like walking stumps, but that one. Well, he understands something about reality. Let's get back to the ship. I want to talk to Sanchez."

Chapter 20

Sanchez and the security team went through the decontamination process without incident. Once cleared by the flashing green strobe, the group headed back to Sanchez's quarters. Nothing was said until the room was cleared of all potential weapons, and they were about to lock Sanchez back in his room.

"Good thing we found you when we did. If one of those creatures would have gotten to you, well, you would probably be a goner," Towers said as he was about to close the door.

"No kidding. Those things would have killed me," Sanchez said with a bit of a defiant laugh.

"Or worse," Towers replied.

"What would be worse than that?"

"If one of them had bitten you. I've heard that all kinds of bad things happen if one of them bites you. Except for what the Captain is going to do to you, you are one lucky man."

When Towers mentioned being bitten, Sanchez's hand instantly went to his arm. He gingerly felt the spot where he thought the creature from the lake might have nipped him. His uniform was torn, and he felt a bit of swelling on his skin.

After the door was closed and the lock engaged, Sanchez bolted to the mirror in his lavatory. He began to whine like a whimpering dog as he strained to pull off his clinging uniform top. Once off, he tossed the garment and jerked his arm up to the mirror.

He examined the area with dread in his eyes. It was all he needed to do. A bite mark was clearly visible. He stared at the wound. *But how bad was it?* The injury looked minor, barely a scratch. *Was the skin even broken?* He couldn't tell from the angle.

Sanchez inched closer to the mirror trying to get a better look. He gazed at the blotchy red mark for several long heart-pounding moments. But if the beast's teeth had broken the flesh, it was so minor it couldn't have affected him.

The Martian stared at the spot a moment longer and then grimaced with apprehension. *"Damn it,"* he barked and then stripped off the rest of his clothes. He set the water temperature as hot as he could stand and then entered the shower. He used a washcloth and scrubbed the wound almost raw.

After finishing, he toweled off and heard a voice at the door.

"A word, Mr. Sanchez,"

"A minute please," Sanchez called back from the lavatory entrance.

"We're coming in," the muffled voice said from the other side.

"A moment please, I'm just out of the shower," Sanchez begged.

Without waiting, Captain Everett had the security man tap in the override code to open the door. As Flynn walked in, Sanchez was pulling on a new shirt. "Thanks for the privacy as I dress," Sanchez scoffed.

"You're lucky I let you have a private room at all. My preference was to have you chained up in the cargo bay for all to see and chastise. What the hell did you think you were doing? Are you mad? Do you realize how that little escapade of yours almost cost you your life? Not to mention a possible lethal contamination from things on this planet. Gary, what you have done is criminal, and there will be consequences."

"I know. It was stupid of me. I admit that my actions were wrong. I am sorry, truly. You made it clear that I couldn't go, so I made a decision to see for myself what was out there," Sanchez said, with only a minor conciliatory tone.

"Yeah, and how did that work out for you?"

"Not so good, I'm afraid. What were those things? I mean, I know they were earthlings, but what was wrong with them?"

"Again, proof of why you shouldn't have done what you did because we have no idea. We can only assume that they have been infected by some rogue pathogen here on the planet. One, I must emphasize, that we haven't had the first chance to analyze. This brings me to you. Did you have any contact whatsoever with those things?" Flynn asked, and there was zero doubt about his expectation for truth.

"Other than being chased and scared out of my wits? No, none," Sanchez replied, though there seemed to be a quiver in his answer.

Flynn eyed Sanchez suspiciously. After a moment of contemplation, he said, "We have guests onboard. Docs going to check them out to see what, if anything, these men's physical presence can tell us about the planet. Once he is done with them, you are next. And I will instruct him to make it a comprehensive examination, so be prepared to have every orifice of your body searched and probed.

After all, we don't want you turning into one of those things, now do we?"

"Huh? What do you mean—turn into one of those things? Can that happen? I mean, we are Martians, not Earthlings. Certainly, we must be immune," Sanchez begged.

"Honestly, we don't know. In the meantime, no matter what happens, you are confined to these quarters. If you try to leave, for any reason, I will have you chained up in the cargo bay with only a bucket to do your duty," Flynn threatened.

"You wouldn't dare."

"Gary, I'm tempted to do it just so you can feel some of the humiliation you deserve. So, don't provoke me in any way, or I'll send you down there so damn fast it will make your stupid head spin off," Flynn steamed, and then spun around and marched out.

"Stony, I'm sorry what I did to you. I was wrong, and I know there is nothing I can say or do to make it up. Just know that I am sorry," Sanchez pled to his guard. When the door closed, and he heard the locking mechanism engage, he reached for the wound on his arm and rubbed it. It was sore. *Did that mean anything? No, it was just a bruise, had to be.* Sanchez stepped back and plopped down on his bed staring into space as he continued to rub the injury.

Chapter 21

"Bobby," Pam Jenkins whispered, her breath lingering around the young radioman's neck, tickling him with intention. "Um, how much longer do ya hafta monitor that thin'?"

"Larry said I needed to stay alert and on point while they were gone, just in case they needed to contact us through the Martian's radio," Bobby replied as the girl's soft blond hair brushed along his neck. The light touch sent a warm rush down his spine and into his groin.

"I wanna get somethin' to eat," Pam said as she stiffened and moved away.

"That's why ya were a'doin that? Thanks a lot!"

"I'm sor—" she started, but then someone raced by the entry of the radio room. The two heard deep winded gasps as the person's footsteps echoed down the stone pathway.

****

When Flynn met back up with Tate and the other earthlings, everyone was back in their respective seats chatting. "I trust you enjoyed your meal. The system provides some great food."

"The system? Ya mean yar cook?" Frank Potter questioned.

"Well, not exactly. You see, the ship has a robotic mess system that cooks everything we eat. We have no chef or cook onboard, though Ms. Canfield can make a mean casserole," Flynn said as he smiled at Melanie.

"Amazin'. I ate the lamb. It was delicious. We haven't had lamb in our colony my whole life," Potter said satisfactorily. With that, Mr. Cummings laughed out loud, followed by the Doctor.

"Wha'?" Potter stuttered. "Don't tell me. That wasn't lamb? I thought ya said it was lamb?" Potter protested to Tate.

"Well, Ms. Canfield told me that all of their *"meat"* is a synthetic product since they couldn't manage a livestock program on their planet. They have done a good job imitating the flavors though, wouldn't you agree?"

"I'll be a son-of—," Potter said with his mouth agape in astonishment.

"So…" Flynn stepped in, "…I'd like to have Doc Carlson run some blood work on your group. Test it with our technology to see if there is anything out of the ordinary."

"But we're not infected. Wouldn't it make more sense to test someone infected?" Terry Peters asked.

"Yes, that will be necessary as well. But if you are immune, then maybe you have something in your system that makes you that way," Carlson interjected. "Besides, we haven't been able to run tests on an Earthling's blood in a long, long time. It is vital that I have a base platform to work with."

"Very well. That makes sense to me. But I also have a few questions if'n I may," Tate said.

"By all means," Flynn replied.

"Based on yar obvious advanced technology, do ya think ya could find a cure for this disease? Though I have no idea about the rest of our planet, I can tell ya that no one we know of has any capabilities or facilities to work on the problem. If'n I would hafta guess, we are not alone in that situation. I think if'n someone had been workin' on a cure and found one, that news would have encircled the globe by this time."

"We can certainly try. And if anyone could find a cure, it would be the Doc and his team," Flynn said as he nodded at Carlson.

"Yes, but I would probably need a live specimen to work with, and that seems a bit, um, problematic, I would think," Doc Carlson added.

"Well, we'll cross that bridge when it arrives. In the meantime," Flynn started to say but was interrupted by his com-link. "Now what?" Flynn said before he tapped his communicator. "Flynn here."

"Captain, we have a situation. Several armed men are by the perimeter shield. Our system saw them coming, but we just thought it was some of those . . . things. However, it doesn't appear to be them. We sent a drone in time to stop them from walking into the shield. They claim they are with Mr. Tate's colony," Lieutenant Grant reported.

"From our colony? Who is it? Did they give a name?" Tate said as he stood.

"Did they identify themselves?" Flynn said as he tapped his com-link again.

"One of them said his name was Bobby Hammonds. He looks pretty beat up sir. As do the rest of the men."

"My God, wha's happened? Bobby Hammonds? How could he have found out where we are? He's never been part of any outside group that I know of. He couldn't possibly find his way around the countryside. I mean, he's our radioman," Potter said stunned.

"Captain, somethin' serious has happened for that young man to have ventured this far from our colony. And if'n they are armed, then somethin' truly dreadful has occurred. Please, we must speak with them," Tate begged.

"Of course. Let's go," Everett offered. He headed around the table but stopped momentarily as he tapped his com-link. "Lieutenant Grant, any sign of our other friends, the hostile ones?"

"No, sir. They've moved off and we stopped tracking them after they were several kilometers away.

Flynn nodded at Tate and then the entire group left the room. Using the closest lift, they made their way to the ship's exit ramp and headed towards the men at the security shield's perimeter. When they arrived, they found five men, all with some wound or injury. Hammond's clothes were ripped in several places, and he had a bandage wrapped around his head and one on his arm.

The dressings looked soiled with blood seeping through. Hank Jacobs, a member of the elders, stood behind Hammonds, with Tom Beacon and Perry Walters behind him. Off to the right was a small thin-boned blond man in his late teens or early twenties. He looked dazed and physically battered.

"My God, wha's happened?" Tate implored.

"Larry, thank the Lord we found ya. We were attacked. Close to 300 men came armed with automatic weapons and assault vehicles. They overwhelmed us and killed so many, so many…" Bobby said, his voice trailing off in obvious despair.

"And our women. Those that they didn't want, they murdered in cold blood. Those they did, well, they tethered them like animals, marchin' them off to Lord knows where. Larry, Boulderside is devastated, completely devastated," Hank Jacobs added. "Somehow, and I don't know how, we haf'ta get our women back. If'n not, we are finished."

"Captain," Tate said as he turned to Everett. "I know ya wanted to have yar doctor check us out, but I must go back to my colony and assess the damage. From wha' my friends are a'sayin, our colony may be lost," Tate said, his voice steeped in dread.

"Of course. We will get you some food and other supplies. Plus, give me fifteen minutes to have the Doc examine these injured men. Looks like most of the wounds are somewhat minor and we have a flesh repair spray that will heal those injuries very quickly. I will also send two of our drones with you. They can report back to my ship so we can assess the situation. And if you decide to go after your attackers, the drones can track them for you," Flynn offered, though he proposed no other assistance with personnel or weaponry. This didn't go unnoticed by Melanie Canfield.

Things ramped up rather quickly with the spaceship's crew racing around to gather provisions for the earthlings. Doc Carlson managed a quick look at the injured colonists and treated what he could treat, though the small blond boy refused to be examined. Flynn instructed Grant and Towers regarding the drone cover. As he watched his crew work, Melanie walked up and spoke. "So, you're not going?"

Flynn didn't look up, "Going where?"

"Going with Tate and his men to see what's happened?"

"Ms. Canfield, at this point of our mission, it would be illogical to accompany their party. As I said, we will monitor their situation with the drones and then decide on a plan of action, if any. After all, fighting in a battle between two factions here on earth is not why we came," Flynn stated firmly.

"Hmm . . . seems to me that the moral and decent thing would be to go there with the Doc and a few of the crew to see if we can be of any help. Doesn't mean we have to go into battle. Just means we are doing what is right to help those who may be injured. Don't you think?" Melanie said matter of fact.

Flynn took in a deep breath and pondered. His brow furrowed as he thought and then a look of resignation washed over his face. He turned and regarded his soon to be wife and science officer. "Now that you put it that way, gather a team and let's give them a hand. Advise the original away team, plus four security men. Also, Doc Carlson, and Mr. Cummings."

"And me of course."

Flynn looked at her, smirked, and said "And you, of course. I will head the team. We leave in fifteen minutes."

Melanie smiled and then turned and rushed off the bridge. Twenty minutes later everyone was assembled, and the group made their way to the security shield. Flynn had the shield opened, the party exited the perimeter, and was soon out of sight of the ship. The hovering drones flanked them on either side, silent and electronically vigilant, as well as one in front of the group by fifty meters.

Moving at a fast clip through a well-worn path, the small troop took about an hour to arrive at the base of the colony's encampment. Along the way, Bobby explained what took place.

"Pam and I were on the radio when someone raced past the room. We only caught a glimpse and weren't sure wha' was goin' on, but whomever it was, was really tearin' it up. We stared at the entrance, not really expectin' anyone else to pass, when three elders scurried by, their faces flushed and filled with fright. A second after they passed, the alarm signalin' a threat to the compound began to blare. Pam and I ran toward the rear escape exit, as we were taught, but others were runnin' toward us. They yelled that the attackers were comin' from that way too."

"They knew about the rear exit? How is that possible?" Terry Peters asked.

"I have no idea. But we weren't askin' no questions at that point and turned around and ran back. When we rounded the corner of passageway three, we bumped into several of our men carryin' weapons. They were bloodied and beaten up. Stan Humphries was with them. He gave me a machete and told me to take Pam and hide. He said they'd wanna take her for sure and to guard her. Scared the hell out of us. We tore off and made our way to the interior water containment area. There's that small cave there where ya cain't see the entrance unless ya know it's there. Pam and I hid there for about an hour."

"While we sat and huddled together, we heard all kinna' terrible noises echoing through the caves. Gunshots, yelling, and God-awful screams that I never wanna hear again. After a while, the commotions began to dissipate until they stopped altogether. When I thought everythin' was safe, Pam and I made our way out of there and tried to get to the main entrance.

"Less than fifty feet down the hallway I ran smack into one of the attackers. I mean ran smack into him. The collision knocked us both down. I banged my head against the wall of the cave—that's how I got this cut on my forehead," Bobby said as he pointed to the nasty gash along his scalp, a wound that still seemed moist and oozing. "I dropped the machete. The guy had a gun, a big one. But before he could raise it to shoot me, Pam picked up the machete and whacked him with it."

"No way?" Frank Potter said in amazement.

"Yeah, she sure'n did," Bobby quickly replied. "The machete went in the guy's neck right here," Bobby said as he took his left hand and chopped it down near the base of his neck, "Blood began gushin' out and streamin' down the front of his chest. This guy was big and tall, way bigger than Pam, or me. He wobbled as he grabbed at his neck. His eyes bulged, and he stared at us like he couldn't believe she did it. He finally fell over, and we ran.

"Once we got outside, I saw Hank, Tom, and Perry fightin' with two men that had captured Sally Coulson. She was lyin' on the ground all balled up, and the five men were beat'n the hell out of each other."

"Bobby jumped right in. One of the guys slashed at him with a knife, caught him a good one on his arm, but it didn't stop him none," Hank Peters chimed in. "He managed to get the bastard with a slash of his own as he countered with his machete. Caught the guy along the top of his leg. It must have sliced through an artery or somethin' because blood started spurtin' out, and he went down. The other guy saw his buddy bleedin' like a stuck pig and just took off. Left him there to die."

"So, where's Pam?" Tate asked.

The whole group turned toward the small blond-haired dirty-faced boy. "Right there," Bobby said.

Everyone turned and stared at the expressionless figure. Bobby's voice lowered, and he explained, "While we sat in the cave, I took my pocketknife and cut her hair as close to her scalp as I could. We wanted her to look like a boy. I took some mud and smeared it on her face and arms. I even cut off her sleeves thinkin' it would make her look tougher. She's got guns as ya' know," he said as they all looked at her arms. But Pam didn't look like she was aware they were talking about her. The girl's face, dirty and smudged just as Bobby said, was blank with no expression.

"I'll be damn," Potter said as he stared at Pam.

"Ya ok?" Tate asked Pam as he walked up to her. He put his hand on her shoulder and asked again, "Pam, ya ok?" But the girl didn't answer; she only stared up at him, eyes glassy and unfocused. After a moment, a tear boiled out of her left eye and rolled down her cheek. She blinked a couple of times, and then offered a shallow nod before moving back behind Bobby.

"She hasn't said much since she chopped up that guy," Bobby offered.

Tate looked at Jacobs, "Who else from the council survived?"

"I don't thin' anyone did. Most everyone was in the council chamber when the alarm went off. I was, um," Jacobs hesitated before clearing his voice and saying, "I was relievin' myself. As soon I heard the alarm, I ran to the chamber and found them all dead. Everyone in the council. The only person I didn't see was Donny Thompson."

Tate turned to Potter, his expression one of alarm. Thompson was Potter's right-hand man. The guy Potter could count on every time he needed someone to come to his aide during an argument. Thompson never had an opinion of his own, but always jumped in when Potter needed a sympathetic cohort.

Some time back, Potter called for a vote for Thompson to be added to the council, but his spineless accomplice was voted down. They didn't want another Potter yes-man on the council. Thompson was pissed—even threatened some elders in the chamber before Potter walked him out and settled him down. Several months later, Potter called for a revote after Bret Felton, an elder and council member, had died. Potter nominated Thompson to replace Felton, and he won out.

But the newly appointed elder caused tension and dissension at almost every turn. He always made an obvious point to support Potter, no matter what the subject matter was. The man was an ass-kisser, and everyone knew it. Even the elders who eventually voted Thompson in regretted their decision. Now, those men were dead, and Thompson was not amongst the deceased.

When Tate, Flynn and the others rounded a small bend the colony's mountain home came into view. Pillars of smoke billowed from several spots in and around the peak and several dead bodies, gored and gouged, could be seen scattered about causing gasps and moans from the five colonists. Though the mountain itself seemed no less for the invasion, other obvious signs revealed utter devastation of the colony itself.

"My God. Oh my God," Larry Tate murmured as he hustled up the trail. "Ted Walters. Bill Smith. Terrance Joseph–please no." The men's corpses littered the ground at the base of the trail leading upward.

Doc Carlson checked the pulses of each of the men on the ground. After a moment he looked up at his captain and shook his head in answer to the veracity of their condition. The ship's crew, none of which had ever seen such chaos, followed Tate in silent dread.

The leader of the community made his way up the trail until they came to a hidden crevice allowing them entry into the cave system of the Boulderside colony. Several bodies littered the pathway in, and Tate checked each one. Dead. All of them.

Survivors of the attack filed out of the entrance, the devastation in their expressions apparent as they beseeched their leader for answers. Tate acknowledged each one by name, assuring them he had brought help. After getting past the alarming difference in the size of the newcomers, each of the injured allowed the ship's doctor to assess their wounds.

Carlson treated those needing care, while the others from the ship handed out supplies and food. One man, somewhere in his late thirties, looked near death. Carlson, sent a medi-scanner to check the man's condition. The scanner, designed to hover in Martian gravity, dropped several inches when the doctor released it. After automatically compensating for the heavier gravity the small unit scanned the body.

The survivors gasped at the sight and watched the gadgetry in amazement. Though references of similar earth made devices had been handed down through storytelling, the sight of the medical device was astounding, unreal even. After a few seconds, the scanner moved back to the doctor, and he plucked it from the air. He studied the small instrument and then retrieved a small cylinder from his tote bag.

He injected something in the man's neck and then waited. The colonist's breathing, which had been random and with gasps, began to even out. He turned to Everett, "The man has some internal injuries. I have stabilized him for now, but he will need surgery. I will call for a transport and have him taken to the ship. I have included a bio-cleanse to make sure that any internal bacterial issues will be cleared before he goes into the external decontamination chamber. That will assure us that no internal contaminant can escape during the procedure.

Everett nodded and then turned to follow Tate. The leader of the colony was now hurrying down the passageway. After about fifty meters, the still visibly upset man arrived at a doorway and froze. The color in his face drained away as he stared at the massacre. When Everett caught up he was taken aback at the devastation inside the chamber. There, lying on the floor, bodies on top of bodies, were twenty or so men. Each appeared to have experienced a violent death. Gunshot wounds, deep gashes and stabs from knives or other sharp instruments, all injuries that would have surely caused death. But, in addition to these injuries a few of the men suffered from battered and crushed skulls. It was as if the attackers were trying to send a message. The savagery was horrific.

Tate walked with unsteady legs through the carnage, his face a composite of grief and outrage. The crumpled bodies lying on the ground were not only the elders of the community; they were his friends, people he had known since childhood. He paused and studied their faces, many of which were covered in blood and bodily fragments. He had suffered with these men through many trials and sufferings. He had laughed and cried and commiserated with most as they all did their utmost to provide the best quality of life they could for their colony.

Everett stood by the door, not moving. He felt for the man, for the entire community. He made up his mind right then that if Tate asked for his help to avenge this travesty, he would give it.

The rest of the men that had accompanied Tate to the spaceship arrived behind Everett. They pushed their way past the taller man and entered the room, each emitting a cry of desperation at the scene. Frank Potter stood with his hands clasping the sides of his face in shock. Terry Peters fell to his knees alongside two bodies and wept. The other two men walked around the room and checked their comrades, begging for them to open their eyes, only to find each one dead. The injuries and bodily devastation too grave for anyone to have survived.

"Somethin' is odd here," Tate muttered in a stilted whisper.

At first, no one responded. Finally, Everett said, "Mr. Tate? What do you see?"

"Of the dead, five have their heads crushed in. Someone used some type of hammer or blunt instrument to bash their skulls. Now, ya could say that maybe only one or two may have had that type of weapon, and therefore others killed the rest with other means. However, two thin's stand out on these five. First, they all have other life-endin' wounds, either a gunshot, or a fatal knife wound, plus the head injury. It almost seems as if'n someone chose to wreak more harm on these bodies than was necessary. Maybe even attacked them after they were already dead."

"And the second issue," Everett asked.

"Each of these men has always had each other's back. No matter wha' the issue, these five always voted the same way. It might be nothin', but I find that a bit strange. No one else in this room has been bludgeoned the same way."

Terry Peters, his head down and his face hidden in his hands, looked up and stared at Tate. After a moment, he stood, wiped away as much of the stream of tears and smoky grime running down his face as he could, and made his way over to where the colony leader stood. Once by Tate's side, he considered the murderous work and shook his head. "Someone had it in for these men. This can only mean that the person who killed them knew them. And if'n he knew them, then he may have been an accomplice to the entire attack."

"Wait, wha' are ya a'sayin'? That one of our own helped these bastards assault our colony. An insider? For God's sake that's insane. I mean, who would do such a thin'," Frank Potter snapped.

At this comment, all eyes turned to Potter, and not because they agreed with him.

———————

"Well, it sure the hell wasn't me. Christ boys, I was with ya the whole time. I couldn't have done this. And besides, no matter wha' ya think of me, I would never, ever, betray our colony!"

"Where is Donny Thompson?" Tate asked the blustering man.

"How should I kn—Hey, wait a minute! Yar not suggestin' that Donny Thompson was part of this? That's ridiculous. Hell, I've known Donny for," He stopped there and thought, "For the better part of twenty years."

"He's not one of us Frank. He never was," Peters said as he took a menacing step towards Potter.

"That's bullshit. Just because Donny wasn't born here doesn't mean he isn't one of us. Hell, he was just a kid when we found him."

"A seventeen-year-old kid. For seventeen years he lived somewhere else," Peters said as he took another looming step toward the now shaking and retreating Potters.

"Look, I know Donny is a pain in the ass, but whatever life he had before comin' here is long since gone and forgotten. It's been almost twenty years!" Potter argued in defense of his friend.

"Take it easy, Terry," Tate said as he put a consoling hand on Peter's shoulder. "Frank, ya'r probably right. Let's just find him. If'n he's here, then we'll know he's not the one. However, whether he's the traitor or not, it is obvious that someone has betrayed us, and we need to figure out who that person is," Tate said.

At that moment Doctor Carlson walked up behind Everett and examined the scene. "Oh my, how utterly barbaric," he said in a whisper.

"Yes," Everett offered as he turned slightly toward the ship's doctor, "This is bad. No need to come in here to check on anyone. These men are all dead." Everett turned back to the room and cleared his throat, "Mr. Tate, is there a way you can call all of your people together somewhere. I think we need to find out how many survived, and how many have been taken.

"I will have several additional members of my crew come here to assist your survivors and help in any way we can. Doc Carlson and his staff should be able to handle most injuries. Then, after we've had a chance to assess the damage and do what we can for those in need, and if you plan to go after the people who did this, I would be willing to accompany you to assist."

"Thank ya, Captain," Tate said solemnly. The man appeared to be teetering on weak knees as he soberly gazed down at his fallen comrades. Suddenly, in a palpable moment of determination, he turned to Terry Peters. "Terry, sound the general assembly horn and have all survivors that can move meet in the great cavern. Perry, ya and Tom see wha' weapons are still here and usable then bring them to the meeting. Once everyone is there, I will address this situation and we can decide, as a family, wha' course of action to take."

Chapter 22

An hour and a half later, 311 frightened, bedraggled, and demoralized people had gathered in the massive cavern. Running rampant throughout the group was a somber revelation. Of the over 600 colonists residing in Boulderside, 112 men and thirty-three women had been killed in the raid. Besides these fatalities, fifty-three men and women had been injured, with some injuries life-threatening. The taken women, some as young as twelve, numbered forty-seven. This revealing information had the throng in a state of barely controlled hysteria.

Tate stepped out on a natural outcropping in the massive cavern and surveyed the scene. He couldn't believe his eyes. Of the 248 men in his encampment just days before, only 136 remained. Of those, twenty-six received injuries from the attack that left them immobile or unable to be part of any team he could use to recover the taken women. Plus, forty of the uninjured were too young or too old to be much help. In his mind, there was no question about whether they should go after the taken. These were family members and friends. There was no other choice. Yet, looking at the battered survivors now huddled in front of him, his hope for success felt more like a smoldering campfire that had been doused with water on a freezing night.

"Can I have yar attention? Everyone please," Tate called out doing his best to quell the multitude of wide-ranging conversations echoing throughout the cavern. Mixed in with the expletive-filled angry dialogues were the sobbing, weeping, and moaning of individuals who either couldn't control their grief or were injured and in pain—or both.

"Please, everyone, can I have yar attention," Tate shouted again. He waited as the multitude finally quieted. The leader of the now devastated community took in a deep breath and with a painful sincerity spoke. "We have all lost loved ones and friends today. I mourn them as ya do. I'm sick for it. Words cain't even begin to express the pain in my heart; all of our hearts. And though we are hurt, exhausted, and mentally beaten, we canna lose sight of those that have been taken. They need us, and we canna' let 'em down.

Tate swallowed hard and gazed with watering eyes toward the colony's ragged survivors. Finally, with barely regained composure and a sigh of resolution, he said, "It would be easy for us to give up and call it a day. Live our last days here on earth as best we can. But eventually, we wouldn't be able to continue, and our remaining family would fade away. We would simply become a waft of dust blowing across the ground, forgotten like so many others. But I, for one, canna simply shrink away and die. Not without at least tryin' to get our people back."

Tate's lips creased in a line of determination. He stepped down from the ancient stone dais and walked through the crowd. As he ambled along, he touched the hands, heads, and shoulders of his comrades doing his best to instill a bond of comradery, hope, and devotion.

"As I walk amongst ya, I will ask each to reach deep within yar very soul's and grasp that small ray of hope because help has arrived. As ya all now know, we have recently been contacted by bein's from Mars—human bein's. These people are direct ancestors from a group of fearless pioneers sent to that planet hundreds of years ago. After meetin' with them, seein' their spaceship, and considerin' their advanced technologies, I believe they may, in fact, be our salvation. These people are advanced in ways we cain't even dream. They have systems and scientific instruments that we could only contemplate with fictional imaginations."

Tate turned toward Everett and his crew and waved a hand in their direction, "Just look at their size and the obvious strength they project. Everythin' about them gives hope that humans can survive the greatest of tests." Tate rotated back and gazed out over the raptured community. He raised his hands in a gesture of embracing everyone in the cavern. "Yes, they brin' us hope. Hope that will help us survive this catastrophic attack and hope that we can get our fellow family members back. But maybe the greatest optimism they brin' is their medical knowledge. Based on conversations I have had with their leader and their ship's doctor; I have a renewed anticipation that they may be able to rid the entire planet of the plague that has devastated its populations."

There was a collective gasp from everyone in the cavern that echoed off the chamber's walls. "Is that true? Can they cure us?" one of the injured shouted from the back of the crowd.

"They are gonna' try. There's no guarantee, but from the stunnin' advancements that I've witnessed on their ship, it looks very promisin'. Everyone, I know thin's look bleak. We've lost much. Yet, with the help of these people, we have a real chance to recover and start anew. We can be stronger and healthier with a potential future like we've never had in our colony's existence," Tate said as he hustled his way back toward the dais.

Facing the group, Tate stood tall with back erect. He said nothing for several long beats. Finally, just as the moment seemed strained, he took in a deep breath and spoke. "Though they are few, these people possess weapons, tools, and mechanisms that we have only seen in books. If'n we are brave, fearless even, we will succeed with their help. So, those of ya that can join our attempt to recover our family members we will be leavin' here at first light tomorrow."

There were shouts of approval and screams of righteous vengeance from almost everyone in the room. Tate held up his hands in a quieting motion. "Not everyone canna' go as we will need people to stay here and attend to those that need our help. We also have crops that need constant attention."

Before Tate could go on, someone in the back of the cavern yelled, "Wha' difference will our crops make if'n we don't have a colony. We need our people back or crops or no crops, we are doomed!" There were more shouts and cries for immediate action against the perpetrators.

"Yes, I know this," Tate responded, "But if'n we are successful, we will need to come back to a community that can still support us. Provisions for the trip are bein' assembled. I have Mr. Peters coordinatin' the mission. He will be at the rendezvous point at the base of the mountain at 6 a.m. Those of ya that will be goin' must be there by then." Tate paused, then after a moment of contemplation, added, "This is a true turnin' point in our survival. If'n we are successful, and our new alliance with our friends from Mars brin's the promise I believe it can, we may not only survive, but thrive. So, until tomorrow mornin'."

Though the Martians were bigger and stronger than their Earthling counterparts, they were by no means warriors in the true sense of the word. Other than sporting events and physical trainings, no Martian had ever been in a combat situation. This mission would be dangerous and frightening for all, and Flynn knew that.

At precisely six the next morning, one hundred and thirty-six people stood at the base of the Boulderside encampment. Frank Potter and Donny Thompson were not among those in attendance. It was decided that Potter was not fit for the trip, and Donny Thompson, as feared, could not be found. He wasn't among the dead nor living, which squarely pointed the finger at him as the traitor to the colony. For what reason, no one could guess, but it had become clear he was the culprit.

Everett moved through the throng, easily a foot and a half taller than the tallest of the earthlings and made his way to where Tate stood. Though Doc Carlson would stay behind and continue to treat the wounded, twelve other Martians followed Everett including Melanie, Brad Cummings, and Marc Antony.

The robot, dressed in a crewmember uniform, brought gasps and murmurs of awe and amazement. Marc Antony was eight-feet tall and proportioned similarly to his Martian owners. His movements were smooth, almost rhythmic, and his facial features were handsome if not roguish. The colonists were stunned. Several drew back in fright. Others, fascinated by the perfection of the being, walked up, and stared up at his face like he was an animal at a zoo.

Each of the Martians was now armed with a laser rifle and pistol. Three drones hovered above them. Another three had been sent out to begin the search for the attackers, though the offending troops had made no attempt to cover their retreating trail. They had little or no fear of a counterattack by the surviving Boulderside residents. So, subterfuge of their escape route wasn't considered.

"The drones will find their forces in short time. They can cover a vast expanse very quickly. Once they find the group, they will hover a couple of thousand feet above them and monitor their movements. The remaining drones we have with us will guide us while protecting our flanks as we go. Once we find these men, we will set up a perimeter defensive position. I will then radio my ship and have it fly to our location. And though the drones have lasers, the ship does not have weaponry, but it is rather intimidating," Flynn explained to Tate.

"Thank ya, captain. Then if'n yar ready, I guess it's time," Tate said. He turned to his people and began directing. "Terry, ya, Tom and Brett Jones will work yar way through our forces and instruct them to march in twos behind us. Remind everyone to stay together and keep up. Hank, I want ya at the rear with one of the communication monitors Captain Everett gave us. If'n ya have any issues or troubles, let us know, and we'll halt the march," Tate instructed.

Twenty-five minutes after departing the colony, Everett received an incoming signal from one of the search drones. He held up a small info-pad receiver and tapped the screen. A picture appeared showing their quarry. There were at least three hundred men. They were well armed and had several vehicles with automatic weapons on them. Another grouping of vehicles held what looked like a small cannon. The forces appeared to be breaking camp with people milling about like ants as they loaded their gear and supplies into several trucks.

"Where on earth did they get all those guns? Those automatic weapons must be many years old, and the ammunition? I am stunned," Tate said as he peered at the screen. "Not to mention the many vehicles they possess; how do they operate? They cain't have the ability to manufacture and refine oil and gas? Can they?" Tate knew that Everett couldn't answer the questions, they were rhetorical. But the fact that these murderers possessed such destructive weapons, and his colony had nothing even close, astonished him.

As they watched, a group of about fifty men gathered to one side of the camp. After a few minutes, those men climbed into various vehicles and headed away from the main contingent. Leading this group were two military jeep style cars followed by eight other vehicles. Of those eight, four had automatic weapons mounted to them, and four were fitted with small barrel cannons. "Can yar drone get a closer look at those men in the lead vehicle?" Tate asked.

Everett tapped a couple of icons on the screen, and the men in the smaller force came closer into view. He moved his finger over the lead vehicle and the picture homed in on the riders. "There, that man. Can ya get a look at his face?" Tate said, pointing to a man in the open cockpit's passenger seat. Everett tapped his finger on the man, and the picture zoomed in. "My God, that's Donny Thompson. He's in the lead car. I knew it. That son of a bitch, it was him that betrayed us."

"Where are they a'goin'? Are they headin' back toward us?" Terry Peters asked.

"No," Tate said as he glared at the image. "They appear to be headin' due east, and if'n they stay on that course, they will end up . . .

****

"Thompson, if you're trying to pull a fast one on me, I will personally relieve you of your balls," the man sitting next to Donny Thompson said.

The driver was Colonel Briggs Layton, the commander of the raiding party that devastated Boulderside. A fat man for the times, Layton bore a continual five-day beard, a patchy black matting that ran up his face almost to his eyes. The stubble never seemed to grow any longer or fill in where the bare spots were exposed. He was mostly bald, though under his cap he maintained an impressive comb-over that did a credible job of hiding it. The soldier had bulging black eyes, pug-like, and a large bulbous nose. Big pores covered his face and were speckled with multiple large blackheads. He was a slovenly rumpled sight.

"I'm tellin' ya the truth. Potter told me about the Martians right before he and Tate left to go visit them. Everyone in the colony was talkin' about it. There really are Martians here on Earth. S'posedly, they are descendants from an Earth mission to Mars some 250 years ago."

"Well then, I guess we need to say hello to our alien visitors before they come to say hello to us," Layton said through a sinister smile. With that, the vehicle they were in moved out with the smaller force in tow. Unnoticed, a silent mechanical spy of remarkable construction hovered high above them. The shadowing sphere recorded their every move.

"This is bad. This is very bad. They are a'goin' after yar ship," Tate said as he looked up at Everett.

"Actually, this is good. They are heading away from the larger force, which means we have fewer men to deal with while rescuing your family members. If we do this right, we may be able to get your people back without having to engage these people in any kind of a military skirmish. I hope that before Thompson and his group know what happened, we'll be heading back with every one of their prisoners. Then, once we get your people safe, we will settle up with them so that they will never bother you again." Everett tapped his com-link, "Ms. Grant?"

"Here, Captain," Lieutenant Grant responded from the bridge of the ship.

"Are you receiving the drone feeds?"

"Yes, sir. I have the two combatant forces as well as your group being monitored by the Virtual Status Imagery System."

"Very good. Set in the coordinates of the main force and move the ship within fifteen kilometers north of their position. By the time the smaller group realizes you are gone, we'll have made our presence known to the others. Keep a close eye on them though, in case they can communicate between their two camps," Flynn ordered.

"Aye, aye Captain. Just one thing," Grant said.

"And that would be?"

"Well, we have another large group heading our way."

"You're kidding? Who are they?" Flynn asked in confusion.

"Well, if I were a betting woman, and because the entire mob is moving like a herd of drunken sailors, I'd say it's our flesh-eating friends coming to pay a visit. Looks like close to two hundred of them. Men and women this time."

Flynn looked at Tate who looked back at him with the almost identical perplexed expression.

"Their estimated time of arrival to your location?" Flynn asked.

"One hour eleven minutes," Grant responded.

"Estimated time of arrival for the raiding party we were following?"

"One hour and twenty-three minutes, give or take."

"Interesting," Flynn said as he looked at Tate. "Could be another bit of good fortune for us." He tapped his com-link, "Ms. Grant, proceed with your instructions. Get back to me once you arrive at your designated location. Everett out."

"Mr. Tate, because we can move rather quickly, I am going to take five of my people and make our way to the designated landing spot of our ship. I want to be onboard when the larger force arrives. I have a plan that I believe will allow us to get your people back safely before you can arrive. If I am successful, none of your forces here will have been put in danger," Everett explained.

"That seems crazy. Ya'll be outnumbered by two hundred to one?" Tate confessed.

"Maybe, but I like my odds. Mel, you, Marc Antony, Brad, Jenkins, and Johnson will be with me. The rest of our team will stay with this group in support, with officer Wells in command. Program one of the drones to lead us, and the rest to stay with this group," Flynn commanded.

Everett and his team of five readied themselves before he turned to Tate once more. "Okay, Mr. Wells will keep his monitor on so you can follow our progress. Keep moving at the best pace you can. If we are successful, then you will know it, and you can stop and wait for our return. If not, we'll go to plan B."

"Wha's plan B?" Tate asked.

"I'll figure that out if plan A doesn't work," Everett said with a wink. "Good luck and see you soon."

Flynn turned and raced off with his team on his heels. Tate and those close by watched them go, slack-jawed and in total awe. The speed at which the Martians ran seemed superhuman, which to a degree, they were. Due to their natural size and strength, and the gravitational cocktail injection that Doctor Carlson had developed and administered to the entire crew, the Martians moved at an incredible speed and for an extended period without resting.

Everett wanted to flank then pass the large attack force without be seen or heard. He had the ship's drone plot a course that would give them a wide enough berth to accomplish that goal. Based on the drone's calculations, and the speed in which his team was capable of, he believed he could meet the ship at the pre-determined location in four hours – it took three and a half.

Once the drone alerted Everett that his team was past the armed forces, the six-man team shifted their course and headed to the now relocated spacecraft. Forty minutes later, breathing heavy but not physically spent, Everett's team arrived at the perimeter shield. The captain tapped his com-link. "Ms. Grant, open the shield," and with that, there was a visible disturbance in the shield allowing them to enter. His team raced up the gangway and entered the decontamination room. Ten minutes later, they were at their respective stations.

Now sitting in the captain's chair and recovered from the vigorous run, Everett surveyed the movements of all parties being monitored on the Virtual Status Imagery System. "Ms. Grant," Flynn said, "Have the drone focus in on that command vehicle," Flynn said as he pointed his laser-pointer toward the lead truck at the front of the main enemy force. Grant tapped her screen and the image magnified. The men in the vehicle wore uniforms with some type of Army insignia on them.

"Run those emblems," Flynn instructed.

"Already done sir. Nothing in our data banks match what they are wearing. Must be post-2057 symbols," Grant said.

"Ok, let's make our presence known. Take us to a distance of about 200 meters in front of that vehicle.

Chapter 23

Corporal Benjamin Pratt of the Colorado Liberation Army sat in the back of the troop carrier leering at his passengers. Twenty-seven women of various ages sat crammed in the vehicle, terrified and unsure what the future might bring. However, Pratt knew precisely what was in store for these captives, and it had him excited.

Certainly, he would be in line for a turn with one of them. Or, who knows, if he was as fertile as he thought he was, he might be part of the ongoing stud service for his settlement. Hell, soon, he'd be the father of dozens of little brats. They would never know he was the father, but that was *ok* with him.

Boulderside resident Paula Dawson, twenty-seven, sat closest to the Corporal. She was a small woman, as many of the survivors were and had been crying almost nonstop since being captured. The women didn't need to be told why they were captured. It would be for the same reason they were coveted at Boulderside. They were or would be of childbearing age.

Yet most of these women were already with a partner they loved. Some already had a child by their mate. But now, they'd likely see none of their loved ones again. It tore at their very beings.

Paula was one of the lucky women with a child, little Frankie. It took her three years to conceive, but finally, she and her husband, big Frank Dawson, were rewarded for their efforts. Big Frank, though ten-years her senior, was a kind and loving man. She had been happy and believed they would be together for the rest of their lives. The thought of her small family being separated made her moan in agony.

Dawson lifted her tear-filled eyes and looked at the Corporal. He was a smug, disgusting man—wiry thin with long greasy hair parted down the middle. He bore a weathered face, heavily pockmarked, drawn, and ashen. His black beady eyes reminded her of a rag doll's button eyes, no feeling or empathy.

Pratt saw the woman looking at him and stared back at her with unabated lust. "You're a fine-looking little lady," Pratt twanged as he nudged Paula with his foot. "I can't wait to have my time with you. Course, you'll need to wipe that crybaby face off first."

Paula jerked her head away and glared at the rest of the women in the truck. Everyone had the same look, horror at the thought of being raped and mauled by these predators.

The convoy of trucks, two filled with the women from the raid, and seven busting at the seams with the soldiers that carried out the genocide, traveled down what had once been a well-maintained four-lane highway. Today, due to decades upon decades of no upkeep, the crater-filled road was nothing more than a remnant of its previous paved grandeur. Weeds, bushes, and scrubs now sprung up everywhere. Where it was once a smooth high-speed route, the road was now a bumpy unforgiving ride.

There were several other vehicles in the convoy, four with automatic weapons attached, and two with small-barreled cannons. Each vehicle held between ten and fifteen soldiers. Behind those trucks were seven Mine Resistant Ambush Protected vehicles, or MRAP's. Each of these cars carried three or four men, mostly officers.

The entire force was intimidating in its size and firepower, especially since the big war had decimated the worlds military forces many years earlier.

This portion of the pillaging force was led by Captain Raul Dominguez, second in command of the brigade. A ruthless butcher with no moral fortitude, Dominguez had displayed a smile of pure gratification as he had bayoneted dozens of Boulderside victims with wild abandon, stabbing each dozens of times, even though they had already suffered life-ending injuries.

Dominguez and Sergeant "Buddy" Hendricks, his lieutenant and equally as corrupt, rode in an MRAP at the lead of the caravan. They were chatting about the day's great victory, laughing, and bragging of how many each had killed, and how many women they planned to molest once they got back.

"Did you see that big blond? The one with those big titties? I am going to have a good time with that one, that's for sure," Dominquez boasted.

"Oh man, she is a fine one. But a little too broad in the hips for me. I like 'em with small hips and big boobs. That's my style, and I know just the one I'm going after the minute we get back," Hendricks said, and then laughed.

As the car rounded a curve in the tree-lined roadway, they came to a wide-open space, easily a couple square miles in diameter. Directly in their path, about a hundred meters in front of them, was something that they could not believe was real.

"What the—" Hendricks said as he slammed on the brakes. One by one, each vehicle in the procession came to a skidding halt. What happened next astonished Dominguez and Hendricks.

A voice, booming and amplified to ear thumping pulsations, ordered, "You will immediately release the female hostages you possess. You will abandon all vehicles and weapons. If you do this, now, you will be spared and may continue back to your colony. You have thirty seconds to agree."

Flynn swiveled his chair toward Melanie, "Too audacious?"

"Only if they don't buy into it. And if they don't, then what? The ship doesn't have external firing weapons," Melanie said. "Though I must say, if I was sitting where they are now and saw this ship looming in front of me, I'd jump off my vehicle and run home like a scared rabbit. We've got to be terrifying the heck out of them right now."

"Yeah, well that's what I'm counting on. Let's give them another nudge. If this doesn't work, we will send drones to confront them. Mr. Cummings," Flynn said as he turned toward his pilot, "Increase the power to the shield and push it out toward that lead vehicle. Let's raise their hair a bit."

After tapping a few screens and icons, Brad then used two fingers and raised a digital bar icon up on his screen. As he did so, a 3-D image of the ship appeared in front of the captain, and then a band that surrounded the ship moved outward. The crew's attention focused on the viewing screen. Within seconds, dust, dirt, and debris whirled and swirled as the shield moved toward the lead vehicle.

"What the hell is going on?" Hendricks said as he inched back in his seat.

"I don't know. Something is blowing shit all around. What should we do?"

"You're asking me? You're the damn Captain," Hendricks shouted back in panic.

Dominguez looked over his shoulder toward the vehicles behind him. Soldiers had raced up to see what was happening. Their faces struck with fear, and their mouths gaped open, they were made speechless by the spectacle. Just then, the hair on Dominguez's head stood straight up.

"Captain, your hair!" Hendricks railed.

Dominguez spun around and reached his hand up to the top of his head. The soldier's hair stood stiff and straight up as were the hairs on his arms. His whole body began to tingle as if a million ants were crawling over his skin. He frantically rubbed at his arms and legs to rid himself of whatever was burrowing into his skin. It didn't help.

Hendricks stared at the man in disbelief unsure of what to do. Suddenly the lieutenant yelped as he felt an electrical jolt crease through his body. The shields electrical essence, which had hit Dominguez first, now swept over both. "Get out! Get out!" Dominquez yelled.

The two men scrambled out of the vehicle and hopped around slapping at their arms and legs and then feverishly rubbing at their faces and scalps. They were groaning, yipping, and yelping as they bounced around in a buffoonish manner.

"Gentlemen, the sensation you are feeling is the beginning of a process called 'Insolvency.' In just a few seconds your body's molecules will begin to mutate. If I move the Insolvency Ray just a fraction further, your entire force will be dissolved. Your bones, skin, and even your hair will be reduced to a pool of liquid slush," the booming voice said.

"Insolvency Ray?" Melanie chuckled.

Flynn glanced her way and shrugged, "Too far this time?"

"I don't know," she said. "They do look scared, and they're hopping around like bunnies. But wait, I think it might be working. Yes, their entire force appears to be dropping their weapons and running. Uh oh…"

"What," Flynn said as he brought his attention back to the viewing screen.

"The women hostages are running away too."

"Damn. That seems to have worked too well. Ms. Grant, send a drone to them and tell them to stop, along with a team to round them up," Flynn directed. He then tapped his com-link. "Lieutenant Wells?" he said as he watched a drone zip out toward the fleeing women.

"Wells here," the lieutenant responded.

"Tell Tate we're collecting the women. They're all safe. We'll bring them onboard and then come to you. Based on your current position," Flynn said as he studied a map of the two groups proximity, "we should be back to you in fifteen to twenty minutes."

"Great news captain. We'll hold our position, and I'll let Tate and the colonists know."

Chapter 24

Gary Sanchez winced as he scratched at the spot where the thing had bitten his arm. It was driving him crazy. He was reminded of the times his parents had told him not to scratch or pick at a healing wound. But even though he tried not to, he had been scratching at the spot incessantly for the last fifteen minutes.

After he could stand it no more, he sat up in his bed and removed his shirt. What he saw made his eyes bulge in terror. There were jagged lines of green running up his arm from the bite mark. The streaks ran over his shoulder, and down toward his chest.

"My God, what the hell. Those weren't there an hour ago," Sanchez moaned. Dread gripped the man. He jumped up and raced to the door. He banged with his fist and rammed on the intercom. "Help me! I'm sick! LET ME OUT OF HERE!"

Eric Stone sat at his monitor in the security office of the deck. A light on his screen indicated that the intercom in Sanchez's room was being rapidly tapped. He looked at it, shook his head, and ignored the signal. He wasn't falling for any more of Sanchez's bull. Not this time. Besides, he was given explicit instructions. Unless Sanchez's bio-monitor had indicated that he had died, Stone wasn't to go in or even acknowledge him. He switched the icon off.

"Come on Stone, I'm not kidding. Something's wrong with me!" Sanchez yelled as he banged and kicked the door. No one came. His heart raced. Panic quickly overtook all reasonable thought. He was having a hard time concentrating. The horror-stricken stowaway stepped back from the door—eyes blurring and arms heavy as deadweights. His stomach lurched; he was going to throw up.

Sanchez ran to the bathroom and collapsed on the ground in front of the toilet. He just got his head over the bowl when he heaved. It was an intense body-wrenching spasm. Yet only a small flecking of green bile came out. He vomited again. Same result. The straining tremors tore at his gut. His stomach was on fire. He tried to stand. He wanted to look at himself in the mirror. As he rose, he felt a tightening in his chest.

"What's–happening–to–me," Sanchez strained out in a croak.

Grabbing at his chest, he moved to the mirror. Through vision impaired eyes he could barely make out his image, but he thought he could see that the green streaks were now covering the entire upper half of his body, and into the hairline of his scalp. In less than five minutes from when he had last looked, the foreign infection had raged like wildfire through his system.

Chapter 25

Donny Thompson sat in the front passenger seat of the military transport as it rounded a bend in the dilapidated roadway. Based on the coordinates he remembered, the Martian ship would be less than a quarter mile away. If it was as large as he believed it must be, the craft should be seen well before they left the cover of the tree line.

"We're close," Thompson said. "If'n I'm right, the ship will be in a large clearin' about a quarter-mile ahead.

Colonel Briggs Layton straightened up in his seat. "Stop the car," Briggs commanded. "Sergeant, go back and have all the commanding officers meet me here.

The sergeant saluted, jumped from the MRAP, and stopped at each vehicle with the instructions. Within three minutes, Layton's officers were standing next to his vehicle.

Layton stood up. "I want the cannon up front as we enter the clearing. Once we spot this ship, I want those weapon's running parallel to the craft, with each cannon spaced thirty feet apart. The fifty calibers will then be driven in-between those positions. I will be to your right. Once we have made contact, I will give them my ultimatum. If they fail to obey, I will raise the red attack flag. We will let them know we mean business. Be ready. Any questions?" The men shook their heads. "Then let's get at it. We've got a spaceship to capture and some Martians to corral."

Once the men were back in their respective vehicles, the colonel sat back down and nodded at his driver. As they moved slowly down the trail, Layton looked over to Thompson. "Watch and learn how I bring these alien freaks to their knees." Layton grinned with a war monger's satisfaction.

Thompson, however, looked like he was about to puke.

While they had stopped, and Layton was doling out commands, Thompson had stood up on the side of the MRAP craning his neck to peer over the tree line. He had expected to see at least the top half of the spacecraft from there. He had not. It made his stomach lurch.

The lead MRAP, with the trailing military vehicles close behind, rounded one last turn and the large open area that Thompson said would be there, came into view. The field was empty. No spaceship, no nothing. Layton grabbed Thompson by the arm and squeezed. "Where is it?" the colonel demanded.

"I don't know. Maybe this ain't the right spot," Thompson stuttered, looking for a way out of his plight. He knew Layton had a short fuse.

"This is the exact coordinates you gave me. You've been lied to. There are no Martians."

"That cain't be true. Why would Tate and his group leave the colony for nothin'?"

Layton glowered at Thompson and slid his hand down to his weapon. He unsnapped the safety strapped and gripped the handle.

"Wait, look," Thompson said as he pointed to the field. Layton spun his head in the direction Thompson indicated. "Look, there in the field. Do ya see? There are three deep indentations. Those must have been caused by the weight of the ship."

Layton grunted and then motioned for the driver to pull next to one of the depressions. The shapes in the soft turf were symmetrical and looked to be about a foot deep and ten feet square. "Maybe," Layton grumbled. He released his grip on his gun. Thompson hopped out and moved to the indentation. The colonel was about to get out to join him when a terrifying shriek jolted the scene.

Layton and Thompson spun their heads and looked behind them. The cannon and machine gun vehicles had begun to spread out as instructed, but when there was no spaceship, they had halted in a long row. Some of the vehicles with cannons had made it out into the clearing, and some had not. The fifty caliber machine gun trucks were still lined up and back behind the trees. Though there was a lot of commotion from the men in those first vehicles, neither Layton nor Thompson could see the cause.

Suddenly, all hell broke out as machine guns and small caliber weapons fire echoed throughout the clearing. An attacking pack of flesh eating scavengers came crashing out of the trees and underbrush like a disturbed mound of fire ants. They kept coming and coming from everywhere. Layton's forces were caught off-guard. And though the small band of soldiers outgunned the attackers, they had been surprised and were quickly becoming overwhelmed.

At that moment, a group of scavengers burst out of the tree line to Layton and Thompson's right and had spotted the lone MRAP. They lumbered in their swaying manner straight at them. Layton saw them first. "Get us out of here!" he shouted. The loudly barked command scared the young driver. He frantically shoved the car into first gear, slammed on the gas, and popped the clutch. The car lurched forward causing Layton to almost fall out his open door. The MRAP veered right and struck Thompson throwing him backward and he landed roughly on his right leg.

Rolling three of four times, the bumped man finally came to a halt, scratched up and shaken, but seemingly no worse for the wear. He scrambled to one knee and watched as the vehicle sped away. "Wait! Stop! Come back! Layton don't leave me," Thompson screamed in terror. The vehicle neither turned around nor slowed down.

An adrenalin rush of fear gripped Thompson's throat as he scampered to his feet. As he put weight on his foot to run he felt a screaming jolt of pain shoot up his leg causing him to stumble and stagger. He'd twisted his ankle in the fall, and though he at first felt nothing, the pain was now excruciating. Grimacing with every step he moved toward the trees with a dramatic limp. With fear throttling all reasonable thought, he mindlessly looked over his shoulder. "Oh my GOD!" he screamed out. Five ravaged scavengers, teeth exposed and chomping, were almost upon him.

"LAYTON, COME BACK!" Thompson roared. He tried to move faster. Panic for his life made the pain less restricting, but he was still not traveling with any real speed. He hopped, skipped, jumped, and stumbled as he fled his pursuers. The man moved like an out of shape bicycle wheel.

If he could make it to the woods, maybe he'd have a chance. He was only thirty feet or so away—a mere stone's throw. This would be nothing for an uninjured man, yet a mile for one that could barely put his weight down on an injured foot. Sweat poured down his face mixing in with a steady stream of blood from a cut on his cheek. The vile fluid ran into his mouth fouling it with a dirty brass taste.

Thompson reached his hand out toward the trees. He was now less than fifteen feet away. If he could just—a hand grabbed onto his shoulder, then another grasped his arm. Thompson screamed. It was a wail of fright that seemed as inhuman as the sounds coming from those now upon him.

"NO! Get away from me. Let go, leave me alone!" Thompson screeched. The horror-struck man tried to wriggle away from the creature's grasp jerking his arms away and swatting at the seemingly dozens of hands grabbing at him. Another scavenger lunged at his waist, and the wrangling group went down in a cloud of dust. The creatures wasted little time as one of them clamped his teeth into the fallen man's right cheek. The beast's victim shrieked in pain. Then something dug into Thompson's ankle at the Achilles. He felt a huge chunk of fleshy meat get ripped away. He screeched again, a bellowing cry of agony.

The scavengers moaned and groaned as they ravaged the man. Like a herd of voracious lions devouring it's still living prey, the scavengers made growling sounds of satisfaction as they chewed and chomped on Thompson's flesh. In unbearable pain, the wounded man beat at the heinous creatures with his fists, kicked at them with his feet. Anything to get free as his last bit of survival instinct was at its tempest. He happened a glance up and saw a hideously disfigured face looming over him. Blood, his blood, was dripping from the thing's mouth and teeth.

Reaching up, Thompson attempted to use his arm to fend off the attacking monster, but the thing swatted away his try and dove down with his mouth and grabbed onto Thompson's throat by his Adam's apple. With a snarl, the feeding ghoul ripped Thompson's throat open. The betrayer of Boulderside's eyes bulged, and he gurgled and gasped with blood shooting from his mouth and roiling out of the gaping hole in his neck. Thompson stiffened, his eyes rolled back in his head, and then all went black.

Chapter 26

The M453-E made the trip to Tate and his colonists in short order. As the ramp to the ship opened, and the members of the two separated families saw each other, a roar of excitement erupted from both sides. As the women poured down the ramp the men ran toward them. The elation was overwhelming. Tate wept like a child. Potter couldn't stop smiling and clapping people on their backs. The women mingled about, hugging, and kissing loved ones in utter joy. They had been convinced they would never see their people again.

To the side, watching with awe, Bobby Hammonds held Pam's hand. She was still shaken, sullen, and would not leave his side. She trembled, and Bobby glanced her way not sure how to help his friend. The girl cried, with tears pouring down her face. But there was also a small yet noticeable smile on her face. It was the first time Bobby had seen her smile since the attack on the colony.

Tate saw Everett at the top of the ramp. He ran up and greeted him, "Captain, there is no way we could ever thank ya and yar crew enough. If we had somethin' to give ya, anythin' that we could reward ya for wha' ya have done, it would be yars. Today, ya have saved our colony from extinction." Tate grasped Flynn's much larger hand in both of his and shook it vigorously.

"We are pleased we were able to help. Now, we can't fit all of you in our ship, so I was thinking it best to transport the women and the men we can fit back to Boulderside and then come back for the rest of you. It will only take two trips, but we'll get you all back safely," Flynn replied.

"Yes, that is wonderful, just wonderful. One other thin', Captain," Tate started.

"Yes?"

"Ya've done so much already, and I hate to ask. But, well, yar doctor; will he be able to work on findin' a cure for the scavenger disease?"

"If there is any way for us to help our ancestors, we are going do it. I will have the doc do a complete work-up on a few from your camp. A clean version of earth's populace, as it were. But, and I haven't figured this one out yet, the Doc believes we will need to capture one of the infected, so we can isolate the disease at the granular level. Once that's done, we will have a ground zero basis for his work."

Tate grimaced. "Catchin' one will be...interestin'," he said with reservation.

"Yes, well, we will figure something out. Shall we go?" Flynn said.

"Yes. I cain't wait to see the faces on those still at Boulderside when we return. There will be much joy and celebration. I hope ya and yar crew will join us."

****

Guard Eric Stone tapped his com-link. "Mr. Sanchez, I'm coming in with your dinner. Please, stand back from the door." He waited for an answer. None came. He tapped the com-link again. "Gary, are you sleeping?" Stone rolled the cart to the right of the door. "I'm opening the door. And just so you know, I have a Taser-wand. If you give me any trouble, I will use it. You won't be surprising me again. Now step back from the door."

Stone took the wand from his waist and activated it. The wand buzzed to life. He dialed in the code to open the door. The grey composite core slid into the wall. Gary Sanchez was standing directly on the other side. Stone, startled, hopped back a step, and raised the wand. Sanchez didn't move forward. He was swaying back and forth, almost like he was doing some weird dance.

"Are you all right?" Stone asked. "What's wrong with you? And what's wrong with your skin? It's all covered with green streaks?" He took another hesitant step backward.

Sanchez ignored Stone's question. His eyes were mired with a milky green goo and seemed unfocused as if he didn't actually see Stone standing there. The stowaway just bobbed and weaved, staring in his direction but not reacting. After a few odd seconds of this strange deer in the headlight's standoff, Sanchez's head tilted slightly, and he sniffed the air.

"Sanchez, what's wrong with you? Why are acting so weird?" Stone asked. "Maybe I should call the Doc or something. You don't look so good," the guard said, his face scrunched up in confusion. Suddenly, Sanchez's lips rolled back exposing his teeth in a snarl. Without warning, he rushed toward Stone and let out an animalistic screech that startled and shocked Stone. "Stay back. Are you crazy? STAY BACK!"

Stone held the Taser-wand out, his arm shaking and unstable. Behavior like this rarely, if ever, happened on Mars. It unnerved the young Martian.

The maniacal Sanchez came at Stone, hands reaching out, fingers opening and closing like pinchers, mouth chomping. Stone backed up in a rush and crashed into the corridor wall behind him. The green-veined Sanchez was quickly upon him, howling like a wild beast. The Taser-wand stabbed his right shoulder and connected at the collarbone before reflecting off. The wand's shock power should have caused Sanchez to jerk back, but the attacking man shrugged it off without a blink and kept coming.

Raising his arm up in a defensive posture, Stone swung the wand around and back down. He was about to shove the metal stick into Sanchez's stomach when Sanchez grabbed Stone's raised arm and sunk his teeth into his wrist. Stone screamed in shock and pain. But Sanchez didn't just bite Stone, he dug his teeth in and ripped out a chunk of flesh and began chewing it.

Panic mode kicked in. In a desperate move, Stone swung the wand around and shoved the metal stick into Sanchez's chest. The full force of the Taser-wand's power sent the snarling man reeling backward and onto the ground against the far wall.

The security guard gripped his bleeding wrist, spun to his left and ran to his security station. He frantically tried putting in the code to open the door, but it didn't work. He turned toward Sanchez. Though stunned, his attacker seemed to be rapidly recovering. A new torrent of panic slammed through the young corporal.

As blood poured down his arm, Stone hit the reset on the pad and tried the code again. Though his fingers were shaking and hard to control, the door slid open. With a cry of relief, he dashed in, spun to his right, and hit the door's closing touchpad.

From where he now stood, Stone couldn't see Sanchez. "Come on, come on," he begged. The door began closing and was almost sealed when Sanchez's face abruptly emerged in the opening. Had the rabid fiend put any part of his body in the opening, the door would have slid open and Stone would have nowhere to run. For some odd reason, Sanchez didn't seem to know or understand that. The door sealed close, and Stone hit the lock sensor.

Chest still heaving from his adrenal overload, Stone jerked open a cabinet in the rear of the office and rifled through the shelves until he found a first aid kit. He could hear Sanchez on the other side of the door making scraping sounds as if he was trying to claw his way in.

Stone opened the kit and found a large wad of sterile gauze. He took the whole pile and applied it to the wound. He grabbed the medical tape and wound the strip around it. Within seconds, blood seeped through the pad. Looking for more gauze, Stone rummaged through the kit again. He found a small spray canister with the words "wound healer" on it and removed the seal at the top of the canister. Just then, a loud banging on the door startled him. He spun around and pressed his body against the back wall in reaction.

The intercom chimed, "Stoney, are you alright? Your door's locked and there's blood all over the—hey, Sanchez, what are you doing out of your—"

"LOOK OUT! There's something wrong with Sanchez. He's crazy. He just took a bite out of my arm," Stone screamed in warning.

There was a shout and a yelp on the other side of the door. Stone was frozen in place. He heard a thump, a bang, and a small crash, and then things went silent. Glued against the wall and staring at the door in horror, Corporal Arnold Stone couldn't move. Finally, with the lapsing of time grinding on his shattered nerves, he took in a breath and inched his way to the window of his station.

As he got to the edge of the glass, he stopped and grimaced. Stone didn't want to look but knew he must. He peeked out. Someone was laying on the ground, and Sanchez was on top of him. Stone couldn't tell what was happening. It looked like Sanchez was whispering something in the person's ear. Eric tapped on the window, "Hey, Sanchez. What are you do…"

Sanchez jerked up and turned his head toward Stone. His face was covered with blood, and there was a large chunk of flesh hanging from his mouth.

"Oh, my God," Stone sputtered as he took a stumbling step backward. Sanchez's face abruptly smashed into the window. His mouth chewed and chomped against the glass. Blood smeared the window.

At that moment, Ensign Rene Henderson came walking down the opposite corridor from where Stone's office was. She stopped in her tracks as she saw the body on the floor and Sanchez clambering to get in through the security office's window.

"Hey, what's going on here?" Henderson said.

Stone saw her, their eyes locked, and then he yelled, "RUN!"

Henderson saw the look of terror on Stone's face. There was no hesitation, she turned and ran. Seeing Rene had shaken Stone out of his fear-induced fog, and he reached over and hit the red alert icon on his security office control panel. A screeching siren blared throughout the ship. Sanchez's head jerked around, searching for what or where the noise was coming from. He caught sight of Henderson as she was tearing down the hall. He screeched that same terrifying scream he had wailed earlier and chased after her, swaying like a windblown flagpole as he went.

"Stone, it's Captain Flynn. An alarm was set off from your station. Did you initiate it?"

Stone tapped his com-link. In a rapid-fire manner that was hard to understand, he spewed, "Yes sir, it's Sanchez sir. He's gone crazy. He attacked me when I brought him his dinner. Then he attacked Ensign Barnes. At least I think its Barnes. Sanchez was eating his face, so I'm not sure if its him or not."

"Hold on. Slow down. Now, what are you talking about? Who was eating what?"

"Sorry sir," Stone said. He took a deep breath and started again. "When I opened Sanchez's door to give him his dinner, he was right there. His shirt was off, and he was swaying back and forth, staring at me with hollow eyes. His body had these green streaks running all over. I asked him what was wrong, and it was like he didn't hear me or understand what I was saying. Then he sniffed the air. It was like he had caught some kind of scent or something. He let out a screech like that of wild beast, and that's when he came at me. It was terrifying. I tried to wand him, but I only caught his shoulder a glancing blow. It shocked him, I'm sure of that, but didn't slow him down."

"Are you hurt; did he injure you?" The Captain said with urgency. Tate, standing nearby and hearing most of the conversation, came rushing over.

"Did he bite him?" Tate asked.

Flynn held up his hand.

"Sir, Sanchez bit my wrist! Took a big chunk right out of me and began chewing it. I mean, he was eating me," Stone said gasping.

Flynn looked at Tate. Tate's eyes were wide, and he began slowly shaking his head back and forth. "Stoney stay where you are. I'll have Nurse Jones look at the wound in a few minutes. Can you stop the bleeding?"

"Yes, sir. For the most part, anyway. I found a first-aid kit and covered the wound with a large gauze wad. Then I found a wound healing canister, and I'm about to spray the wound. I lost a good deal of blood, but I think I'm ok."

Chapter 27

"This is the Captain. The alarm you are hearing is **NOT** a drill. Gary Sanchez is loose on the ship. He has contracted a highly dangerous disease and is very contagious. We are running a bio scan to locate him, but if you see him first, do not try to apprehend him. Immediately seek shelter, lock yourself in, and report his whereabouts. I repeat, he is highly contagious, and you must not confront him."

****

The form of Gary Sanchez lumbered down corridor B2; his craving to feed consuming his now limited mental functions. The voracious virus that resided in his brain had targeted parts of his cerebrum that controlled all reasonable human moralities and had left him with a simple single goal, to feed. He let out a guttural snarl and sniffed the air.

A door opened to his right. Sanchez saw the sliding core disappear into the wall, yet all understanding of someone traversing in or out of the opening had evaporated from his mind. As he stared at the spot, a cart rolled out with medical items on it. Pushing the cart was a tall muscular blond woman dressed in a white jumpsuit. The woman's uniform had a name tag stitched on the right side of her chest, it read, Jones.

Startled, Nurse Jones instinctively pulled the cart back. "Sorry," she said. At that moment the captain's message began over the ship's speaker system regarding Sanchez. Before the warning finished, the infected man lunged at Jones. The nurse, large in both height and physical stature, even by Martian standards, pushed the cart hard into Sanchez and knocked him off balance. The charging attacker crashed into the corridor wall to her left and fell to the floor. As she turned to go back inside the sick bay, Sanchez shot out a hand and grabbed her by the ankle.

"Oh no you don't," Jones said. She lifted her other foot and kicked Sanchez square in the face four times. The heel of her shoe smashed into his nose, his mouth, and into his forehead, putting a large cut across his scalp. A greenish red-hued flow of blood began flowing from the wound.

The nurse's onslaught should have slowed Sanchez, at least a bit, but the man didn't react as he should have. He just continued to growl and pull at her leg. All through this melee, Sanchez's teeth were chomping wildly making terrible clacking sounds with every chomp. Jones continued to kick at Sanchez until a coating of sticky blood, or at least she thought it was blood, covered most of his face.

With the captain's alert still ringing in her ears, Jones wrangled her body and squatted down to hit the attacking man with her fist. She smashed him a few times in the face and heard a snap and a crack as the prone man's nose broke and slid sideways. Again, this physical damage did little to slow Sanchez's efforts.

Now frantic, Nurse Jones rose into a standing position. She raised her left leg high into the air and then slammed her heel down on the wrist of the hand holding her ankle. This time, the loud crackle of breaking wrist bones caused Sanchez to let go. As Jones frantically stepped back and out of Sanchez's range, she tripped over the cart and lost her balance. Her arm flew up, and she hit herself in the face with the back of her hand.

A large smear of Sanchez's blood went into her nose and across her eyes. She desperately scrubbed at them to wipe away the sticky smudge. Sanchez took the moment to get back on his feet. Through clouded vision, Nurse Jones saw Sanchez's form looming and didn't wait for his next attack. She jerkily stumbled her way backwards and into the sick bay tapping the door closing icon as she went.

As the door shut, Sanchez roared with a guttural growl of disapproval. He slid over and banged on the door with his good hand in wide club-like swings. It was a feverish maniacal attempt to get at his prey. And then, like his mind forgot that Jones was even there, he turned and walked away.

As he plodded off, his breathing rasped as fluids from his broken nose leaked into his throat and lungs. His wrist, smashed by Jone's ferocious kick, flopped back and forth in a sing-song motion. And though the damage from both injuries should have caused excruciating pain, Sanchez showed no outward signs of agony.

****

"Stone, it's Lieutenant Grant. You ok in there?" Security officer Belinda Grant said as she knocked on the guard room's door. There was no answer. She looked through the viewing window, smudged with a green-red goo, and saw Stone sitting in a chair, his eyes closed. The ship's alarm continued to blare, loud and ear piercing. She tapped on the window. Stone remained unmoving. She tapped harder and called out his name. Stone's eyes slowly fluttered open. She waved at him.

"Stoney, you ok?" Grant mouthed through the glass.

His head nodded slightly, though that minor exertion showed great strain in his face. When he attempted to stand, this also appeared to demand great effort. He slogged over and attempted to put the unlock code into the door's sensor pad.

The first attempt failed, and Stone shook his head in confusion. He tried again. Grant watched and saw that the ensign was having a difficult time remembering the code. Finally, on the third attempt, the door opened.

"Stoney, where's Barnes?" Grant asked when she walked in.

Stone looked at her confused. He closed his eyes in thought and then looked down at the ground where he remembered that Barnes had been laying after the attack by Sanchez. "He was right there," the corporal said pointing with his hand, though his words were somewhat slurred. Stone's face seemed to morph and skew. "I mean, I think he was. I'm a little confused. Can't think straight for some reason."

"Let's get you to sick bay," Grant said. Ensign Tony Greives and Petty officer Rich Johnson were with the security officer. The three escorted Stone down the corridor toward sick bay.

"My legs and arms are so heavy," Stone groaned. "I can barely walk. And my chest is tight, feels like someone is sitting on it."

"We're almost there. You're doing fine," Grant said as she took an arm to help him, being careful not to let his bloody wrist touch her. As they made their way around a turn, they saw a cart sitting in front of sick bay with medical equipment strewn on the cart and the floor. "Strange," Grant said.

The security officer replaced the instruments on the cart and then moved it against the wall. The door to sick bay didn't open on its own, so she tapped in a code on the entry panel. The door remained closed. The group looked at each other in surprise. Grant re-entered the code. Nothing. She pulled a small device from a pack on her hip, tapped the screen, read the info, then entered a security clearance override code in the sensor pad. The door slid open with a swoosh.

The room was veiled in darkness with only a small light shining near the back.

"Lights on," Grant said. The room lit up brightly. Hello? "Nurse Jones, are you here?"

There was no answer. The large medical room was empty and eerily quiet. Then a noise to their left jarred the four and had Grant reaching for her laser-pistol. The sound came from a storage locker.

"Jones, you in there?" Grant demanded. She heard a moan. The security officer nodded at Grieves and pulled her weapon. "Jones?" she demanded.

The door slid open, just a little. "I'm here," Nurse Jones called out, her voice hoarse and gravelly, "Is he gone? Is Sanchez gone?"

"Yes, you can come out," Grant said as she holstered her weapon.

"The light. It's so bright out there," Nurse Jones muttered.

"Lights at fifty percent, "Grant said. The room dimmed significantly. "Put Stoney on that gurney," Grant said to Grieves and

Petty Officer Johnson. "Nurse, you can come out, we've dimmed the light."

Jones' hand emerged from the closet. With a noticeable effort, she pushed the door open and stepped out. The large woman moved sluggishly, her steps plodding as if her legs had heavy weights tied to them. Even with dimmed lights, Grant could see that the nurse's eyes were swollen and mere slits. "What's happened to your eyes? Did Sanchez hit you?"

"No, he didn't hit me," she wheezed. "He attacked me, and I knocked him to the ground. Before I could go back inside sick bay, he grabbed me by the leg. I punched and kicked him. I think I may have broken his wrist because I heard a loud crack and then he let go. When his grip released, I stumbled, and my hand flew up and hit my face. Something wet splashed into my eyes, and now I can barely see."

"Let me take a look. Come a little closer to the light," Grant instructed.

"It hurts."

"Just a little closer. I need to see."

Nurse Jones shuffled a few feet into the light. Grant took in a shocked breath.

"What? What is it? What's wrong?" Jones begged.

There were streaks of green radiating from her eyes and nose racing towards her scalp and down her face and neck. "You've been infected. We have to put you and Corporal Stone into the quarantine chamber."

Jones began to cry.

"Lieutenant, we've got another problem, "Greives shouted, "It looks like Stone is going into cardiac arrest or something.

Chapter 28

"Captain, we've got to get my people off the ship, and now. If yar crew has been infected, and it's not put in check quickly, every person on board will be plague-ridden so fast that within days all will be lost. This disease can be transmitted in so many ways. It can even become airborne. If it somehow gets into yar ventilation system, it will be too late for any of ya," Tate said.

"Okay. Ms. Canfield," Flynn said to Melanie, "Make it happen. Give them as many supplies as we can spare. Alert me as soon as they've cleared the ship. We need to get the Doc."

Flynn made his way back to the bridge. Once in his chair, he tapped his com-link. "Doc?" he said.

The com-link system had a unique identifying process. It detected who was speaking and whom to contact based on a sensor chip in the brain. Everyone on Mars had the chip implanted at birth—the electrical energy from the brain provided the sensor with a perpetual source of fuel. Once a person was old enough, they began wearing a com-link communicator, two sensors, the one in the brain, and the one in the communicator, paired. From then on, the person could contact anyone on Mars if they were wearing their own paired com-link.

"Carlson here," the Doc answered.

"Doc, what is the status with your task at the colony?" Everett asked.

"We're pretty good here. All the wounded have been tended to with significant results. The inhabitants react very well to our medications."

"Good. We are on our way back. Unfortunately, we have a situation of our own. It seems that Mr. Sanchez was sickened by this strange virus while on his little jaunt outside of the ship. Now, it appears he has infected others. We are on our way to pick you up. You need to go to that clearing southeast of the colony. We will be there in twenty minutes. Everett out."

****

"Jones, help us!" Grant said frantically as she attempted to provide CPR to Stone. She was compressing his chest and was about to go to his mouth when just inches away she stopped. She turned to the Nurse, "Get over here and do something. He's infected, I can't put my mouth on his. Use one of your ventilators or something and help him!"

"I'm having a hard time thinking, for some reason," Jones said vacantly. "And I can't seem to lift my feet to walk. They're so heavy. I can't see so well either," Jones continued, her voice thin and weak.

The nurse's eyes looked like a swarm of bees had stung them repeatedly. Her puffed-out eyelids bulged as if they'd been inflated. Green slime puddled around the corners. Grant couldn't even tell if she was looking their way or not.

Stone's body suddenly stiffened straight out, his head jerked back, and he was so unyielding that Grieves and Petty Officer Johnson had a hard time holding him on the gurney.

"We have to do something," Grant said. Stone shook and flopped; his whole body vibrated like an out of sync gyro. Grieves and Johnson held on for dear life—his strength was almost superhuman.

As if hit by an electric jolt, Stone's eyes bolted open. They were glassy with a green-hued film coating them. His body relaxed, and he went still. Nothing happened for several seconds with Stone staring at the ceiling.

"He seems to be a little better," Johnson said as he glanced at Grieves.

"I don't know. His eyes look strange. Maybe we should get some restraints or something while he's calmed down," Greives said.

Stone, eyes still staring straight up, took in a long breath followed by three short sniffs. A low growl crawled out of his throat. Without warning, he bolted up and sank his teeth into Johnson's neck. The Petty Officer screamed and jerked back. Flesh ripped out of his neck and blood spurted out. Stone's deep bite had nicked Johnson's right external jugular.

Grant and Grieves shuffled back with Grieves slamming into Jones. The nurse, seemingly unaware of anything, crashed over a table spilling its contents all over the floor. She toppled over the table and landed on her back on the ground.

Stone, mouth voraciously chewing Johnson's flesh, heard the crash and turned his head toward the other three. As if warning them to stay back from his kill, he scowled at them and issued a threatening growl. This harsh throated sound was different than what they heard before. This time, the noise was more menacing, a guttural snarling sound of warning. Once Sanchez's intentions were clearly conveyed, he turned back toward Johnson.

The young Martian petty officer was on his knees doing his best to stem the flow of blood, but the gooey metallic-smelling fluid oozed between his fingers unabated. He gagged, gurgled, and collapsed to the floor in a fetal position.

Stone, face and neck slick with Johnson's blood, swallowed what was still in his mouth and then clamored down to the floor. At first, it seemed as though his legs wouldn't hold him up. They buckled and he teetered before making an awkward move toward Johnson, lips curled, teeth exposed, and mouth chomping up and down like a wind-up toy.

But before he could reach his prey, a high piercing blast rang out, and an instantaneous streak of blue light rocketed into Stone's back. The force of the ray slammed him against the wall like a tossed rag doll and he collapsed into a heap, smoke rising from the wound.

"Jones help Johnson. Jones," Grant shouted at the dazed nurse. She was still on the ground, slits for eyes and not moving. Suddenly, her body went rigid and began to shake and gyrate, just as Stone had done moments before. Her head shot back in a snap, and her eyes rolled back in their sockets. "My God," Grant gasped.

Grant and Grieves stood like statues as they looked back and forth between the writhing Jones and the gurgling Johnson. The pooling fluid now forming around the petty officer was a mixture of red blood, and what looked like streaks of green slime.

Stone, who at first appeared dead from the laser's blast, stirred. "How can that be?" Grieves shouted. "He took a direct-kill laser blast right in the center of his back. He should be dead, dead, dead!"

"Out. Out now!" Grant ordered. Grieves didn't need to be told twice. He turned and raced out of sick bay with Grant right behind. Once they were out and the door was closed Grant tapped in a new security code on the entry pad that could not be opened from the inside.

"Captain," Grant huffed, after she had initiated her com-link.

"Everett here."

"Captain, things are spiraling out of control down here. Stone turned into one of those . . . things, and I believe Nurse Jones has too. Stoney bit a huge chunk out of Petty Officer Johnson's neck. He's like a wild animal. He was about to attack Johnson again when I blasted him with my laser pistol; it was set on kill. He was slammed into the sick bay wall by the shot and crumpled to the ground in a heap. He was dead, I was sure of it. I was moving to help Johnson when Nurse Jones started going through some type of seizure. I didn't know who to help first. But before we did anything, Stone began to move. It doesn't seem possible, but somehow, he survived that direct blast."

Grant took a breath and sighed heavily before adding, "Sir, the good news is Jones, Stone, and Johnson are now locked in the Sick Bay. The bad news is..."

"That Jones, Stone, and Johnson are locked in the sick bay. Yeah, that is bad since we need Doc to go there as soon as he gets onboard. Ok, we'll figure that one out in due time. What about Sanchez?"

"I have no idea where he is. I'm heading to the security office to do a ship scan now."

"Let me know as soon as you locate him. We need to isolate him right away. We can't afford any more of our people being infected."

"Uh, what if he won't let us isolate him?" Grant asked, knowing that her Captain would understand her meaning.

"Do what you have to do to safeguard the ship and crew. Everett out." Flynn turned his attention to the front viewing screen, "Commander Parks, ETA for reaching the Boulderside team?"

"Eight minutes," Parks answered after viewing their progress.

"Doc," Flynn said into his com-link.

"Yes Captain," the doctor responded.

"ETA is a little less than eight minutes. We've had to leave the group from Boulderside behind. They are walking back. Please advise their people. When we land, I will meet you at the decontamination chamber and brief you on what is happening. Mr. Tate has warned me that—"

The alarm, which had gone from the blaring audio alarm to flashing red lights, reverted to the blaring alarm again.

"Mr. Parks, what's happening?" Flynn demanded.

"Sir, there were three alarms activated in corridor's B2, B3, and B6," Parks answered as he glanced with confusion at his console.

"Who set them off? Is it a malfunction?"

"No sir, the system is working properly."

Security Chief Grant interrupted through Everett's com-link, "Captain. We have more reported cases of the virus. Three separate people in three different locations have begun to go through the stages of mutating.”

“How? Did Sanchez attack three more of the crew?”

“No sir. The affected have not been in contact with Mr. Sanchez,” Grant said.

Flynn looked around the room and settled his gaze on Melanie. “It’s airborne,” Melanie stated without being asked.

“Captain? Is everything ok? I thought I heard the security alert,” Doc Carlson said through the com-link.

“Doc, Ms. Canfield believes the virus has gone airborne. Three more of the crew have been infected, though none have had any direct contact with Mr. Sanchez. Suggestions?” Flynn asked.

“We’ve got to isolate all the infected and redirect the air filtration system to bypass that quarantine. Then find a way to clear the air from the virus in the rest of the ship. I believe there is a way to reverse the filtration system, suck out all the infected air, and then replace it with treated air. The only problem.” The doc hesitated here.

“The only problem is that you need to find a way to kill the infection to make all of that happen,” Flynn interjected.

“Yes sir. I need the sick bay cleared. Then, I suggest that Marc Antony assist me with the work, since he can’t be infected. I’ve got blood samples from several of the wounded. I’ll need a sample from one of the diseased onboard. Preferably Sanchez since he was directly bitten by one of the beings here on Earth. I’ll need an oxygen system for myself, with several back up tanks, as I will need to work around the clock on this,” the doc said.

"Ok. We'll be ready when you get here. ETA now three minutes," Everett said and then he tapped off his com-link.

"Uh, Flynn," Melanie started, "I don't feel . . ." and that's all she got out.

Chapter 29

"Melanie!" Flynn shouted as he jumped from his chair. Marc Antony, who was only a few feet away, reacted with lightning speed and was at her side catching her before she hit the ground. The android laid her gently on the ground and stepped away so Flynn could tend to her. His fiancé was conscious but struggling.

"What's wrong? Tell me what's happening," Flynn said as he cradled her head in his lap.

"I'm not sure. I was looking at a few read-outs on my monitor when I got light-headed. My throat felt thick like it was closing, and my vision began to blur. The next thing I know, I'm falling toward the ground. My legs and arms feel like they weigh a ton. Flynn, I'm scared. Do you think I'm infected?" Just then, a technician at one of the other workstations keeled over and landed face-first on the bridge's floor.

Brad Cummings, trying to stay focused, brought the ship into the clearing where Doc Carlson and his group stood. "Captain, we've arrived at the rendezvous point. Doc and the others are there. Should I open the bay doors?"

"No, we can't take a chance. If the doc gets infected, we are finished. We'll have to do the best we can to set up a sterile lab at the landing site,"

Still holding Melanie gently in his arms, Flynn tapped his com, "Doc?"

"Yes sir," Doc Carlson responded.

"Doc, things are progressively getting worse here. Crew members are dropping like flies. Melanie just collapsed here on the bridge, as has Lieutenant Powers. I'm not sure how long before they turn, but I'm being told it's rather quickly. Once the ship is secured, I am going to send all nonessential personnel to their quarters. Lock them in till we figure this out.

"I think it best if we set up a portable lab with a purified oxygen system for you on the planet's surface. Please send over a list of items you will need. Flynn out."

Flynn looked down at Melanie and moved a strand of hair from her face. "Hang in there Mel," he said with love and concern in his voice. He tapped his com, "Ms. Grant. What's the status of Mr. Sanchez? Have you found him?" Several seconds went by with no reply. "Ms. Grant, please report." There was urgency in his voice. Grant was head of security, and he needed her. He looked down at Melanie, and then toward Brad. Flynn grimaced just as his com-link activated.

"Sir, its Security Officer Jenkins. We found Sanchez. Officer Grant has him cornered and is . . ." Jenkins hesitated.

"And is doing what?" Everett demanded.

"Captain, she's herding him toward a crewman's quarters with her laser. She's set the weapon to stun, though when she fires at him it only pushes him in the opposite direction of the beam. So, she keeps zapping him along like she was using a cattle prod from those old westerns. Hold one sec sir," Jenkins said. "Ok, Mr. Sanchez is inside the room and the door is sealed."

"Grant here, sir. Sorry I couldn't answer you back earlier. I was a little pre-occupied," Officer Grant said.

"Understood. From what I can determine by the various warnings and alerts, this thing is grabbing our crew at an alarming rate. Ms. Bradshaw and Mr. Powers are down here on the bridge as are others around the ship. I'm not sure how long the gestation period is but we've got to assume it's fast and they'll soon turn.

"I'm going to announce that all nonessential personal must go to their quarters immediately. I want you and your men to provide food provisions and then lock them in with the override code. After those personnel are secure in their quarters, we should have a skeleton crew of around twenty still on station. Each will have to be constantly monitored. We will have their bio-scans set up to alert us of any changes to their chemistry.

"Dr. Carlson is sending over a list of items he will need for his outside lab. Which means, we will need to secure sick bay. Let me know when you have the designated crew locked in their quarters and then I will meet you at sick bay. Can you accomplish this in say, twenty minutes?" Everett asked.

"Aye, Captain. I'll get it done," Grant said, and then signed off.

"Brad, Mr. Anderson, and Mr. Banders, with me as we assist Ms. Bradshaw and Mr. Powers to their quarters," Flynn said as he helped Melanie stand. The woman was limp as she leaned against his shoulder. Her face was pale with beads of sweat on her temples and forehead. Flynn grabbed her arm with Brad on the other side doing the same. Marc Antony moved close to help.

"M.A., I need you with the doc. Head there now and give him all the assistance you can. We've got to get a handle on this and fast," Everett said.

Marc Antony nodded and left the bridge.

Once Lieutenant Powers was safely in his quarters and the lock code was inputted in the door panel, they made their way to Melanie's room. After they laid her down on her bed, the other officers went outside leaving Flynn sitting next to her.

"What's going to happen now?" Melanie asked in a hoarse whisper.

"Doc's going to find a cure, and all will be well," Flynn responded confidently.

"No, I mean, what's going to happen to me? Will I..." Melanie stopped in midsentence, the words getting caught in her throat. A tear ran own her cheek. Flynn gently wiped it away with his thumb. "Promise me that you won't let me hurt anyone. Even if you have to kil—"

"Stop it! Doc will get this thing under control, and you'll be fine," Flynn assured her, though the words didn't portray his inner voice that was screaming in anguish.

"Captain," Grant's voice came over Flynn's com-link.

"Go," Flynn responded.

"I'm at sick bay. I've tied into the cameras inside the clinic, and I can see Nurse Jones and Stoney inside, as well as Ensign Johnson. Johnson is on the floor and he's—well he's pretty chewed up. He's got a huge chunk of flesh missing from his neck and several gouges in his face and head. One of his ears is missing as is most of his left hand."

"My god. Ok, I'm on my way. Grab sidearms for four. I've got Commander Cummings as well as Ensign's Anderson and Banders with me."

"Aye Captain. I'll send one of my security officers to retrieve the weapons.

****

"Let's see them," Flynn said to Grant when he arrived at sick bay. Grant brought up the cameras on his info-pad. The Martian scavengers were milling about, moving around the rooms with seemingly no obvious purpose to their activity. Medical equipment had been knocked to the ground and several tables had been overturned, but it didn't look like the clinic had been too badly disrupted.

"They've just been moving around like that since we got here. It's like they don't know what to do. They're just ambling around in mindless circles," Grant said.

"We've got to get in there, so we need a plan of attack," Flynn instructed.

"Going to be interesting. As I said, I hit Stone dead center with a kill blast from my laser-pistol. He went down, but within five minutes, he was moving again."

"Tate said that the only way to be sure you kill these things is to destroy the brain. To do that you would need to sever the spinal cord at the neck, shoot the infected in the head, or remove the head completely. I can't do any of those things to our crew. I'm hoping Doc will find a cure for those that have been turned. So, we're going to have to stun them again, and then tie them up," Flynn said.

"There are some shackles in the armory. I'll contact Jacobson to bring them along with the weapons," Grant said.

"Captain?" a voice came across the Captain's com-link.

"Everett here, go ahead," Flynn responded.

"Sir, this is Lieutenant Briggs, the bio-scan of Ensign Stewart has just gone haywire. He's left his station in engineering and appears to have moved down corridor C-4 before stopping. It looks like he has fallen down."

"Anderson, Banders, meet Jacobson at the armory. Get two of the laser pistols and a set of shackles then head to corridor C-4. Get Stewart to his cabin, and then get back here. On the double," Everett commanded. The two raced off without a word.

Within minutes, Jacobson arrived with the shackles and weapons. "Ok, let's see where they are again," Everett said as he moved up next to Grant.

"Both Jones and Stone here in the back near bed number's three and four," Grant said as she moved her finger around the info-pad.

"Ok, set your weapons for maximum stun," Everett instructed.

"Ok, Jacobson to my left," Grant said. "Sir, you and Commander Cummings should follow us in. The two of you guard our backs as we move toward the back of the room. We can decide how to subdue the two of them once we position ourselves," Grant said, as she reset her weapon to full stun. "Ready?"

The other three nodded.

"Here we go."

Chapter 30

Security Officer Grant, laser pistol in hand, tapped in the override code on the entry pad of the sick bay. The door slid open, barely making a noise. With Jacobson by her side, Grant moved into the room, crouched with laser pistol up and ready. She hadn't gone in two feet when a shriek that could curdle milk split the air. Nurse Jones had made her way back into the entry area and immediately spotted the intruders. She let out the screaming alarm and began moving toward the two.

Grant, momentarily startled by the reaction of Jones, regained her wits, took aim, and fired. A streak of blue light slammed into the attacking woman, and she went down in a heap. Grant and Jacobson raced over, grabbed the fallen nurse by the ankles, and dragged her out.

"Move it!" Flynn yelled. "Stone is heading our way."

The lumbering Stone saw the group dragging Jones and squealed that same nerve-racking scream and raced toward them.

Grant and Jacobson had almost gotten back to the door with the nurse when Flynn sent a shot toward Stone. The laser blast bit into the oncoming attacker at the shoulder. Stone spun but didn't go down. The round had slowed him, but in a blink he was back on the assault. Flynn fired again. This time, the laser blast hit the junior security officer in the chest, just below the sternum. Stone went soaring backward landing in a heap, unmoving.

"Quick, we've got to get them shackled and into the storage room," Grant said.

Everett hit his com-link, "Doc?"

"Carlson here," the doc answered.

"We've got the sick bay secured and will start gathering all the equipment you asked for." Everett hesitated for a moment. In a voice thick with concern he added, "Doc, I know you have no idea what you're dealing with here, but if you can't come up with something to stop this thing soon, I'm fearful that the whole ship will be compromised."

"Maybe we should have those that have not been infected disembark? Protect them from the contaminant?" The Doc suggested.

"What if everyone is already infected, but just haven't begun to turn? Then we'd have people outside of the ship and out of containment."

"Yes. Well, that is something to consider. Yet, we may have some onboard who are like the inhabitants here. Resistant to the plague or possibly immune. Keeping them out here may take them out of harm's way of those that might still turn and attack."

"Also, a good point. What if you run a blood analysis on those that appear unaffected to determine if they are clear of the infection?" Everett asked.

"Yes, excellent. A Medilyzer will provide a quick blood scan and give us what we need to know. But I think you should test those who seem unaffected there on the ship before letting them come out. If I do it out here, and whether they are told they are infected or not, they may not be too excited about going back in."

"Ok. We'll do the initial testing here and then send each of the unaffected out with a piece of your equipment. I'll alert you when we're going to send out the first group. Captain out," Everett said, tapping his com-link.

Thirty minutes after alerting those crew members still not affected to gather at the loading dock entrance, Officer Grant began analyzing blood samples.

Once Everett was sure that the doc's equipment was staged, and the testing had begun, he headed to Melanie's quarters. He needed to check on her condition. When he got to her door he tapped in the first two numbers and stopped. He took in a breath and then hit the pad's intercom button, "Mel, it's Flynn. Are you ok?" There was no answer. Flynn tried again, "Mel? Are you there? Can you hear me?"

Flynn waited a good thirty seconds for an answer, but no answer came. He couldn't believe what he did next. He pulled his laser pistol and reached over to the door's entry pad. His hand wavered. *I must know.*

He typed in the by-pass code and the door slid silently open.

Flynn, his pistol up, stepped through the door. Melanie's quarters, like those of all the officers on board, had three compartments. A sitting room containing a couch, a small table, and two chairs, was the first room you entered. From there a small hallway led back to the sleeping area. That room consisted of a bed, a nightstand, and a small computer station with a chair. The right side of the room led to the bathroom and clothes closet. Melanie was not in the sitting room.

"Mel, it's Flynn. You ok? Can I come in?" Flynn said in a tone just loud enough to be heard in the back room. A low noise, half moan, half growl, reverberated down the hall. "Mel? Is that you?"

Flynn heard another low guttural growl, deep and throaty like the sound a threatened lion would make.

Flynn inched toward the bedroom. Mel was there. And though he hoped differently, he knew the woman he had loved above life itself would not be the woman in the back room. And then the screech! That now all too familiar wail from a carnivorous being with a single mindset, to feed on live flesh. Flynn scurried back toward the quarter's entry door, laser pistol now clutched in both hands, and pointed down the darkened hall. A tear fell from his left eye and ran down his cheek. He wiped it away with his sleeve.

Flynn positioned himself into a firing stance. He heard a dragging of feet and then a long shadow emerged followed by a hunched figure, moving back and forth in a singsong manner. The form slid slowly from the darkness.

At first, all Flynn saw was the shape, but gradually a face emerged, though it was not the face he remembered or expected to see. This was not the beautiful smiling face of Melanie Canfield, the woman he had fallen asleep next to on so many memorable nights. No, this face was that of a deranged animal. A stalking beast looking for its next meal.

"Oh, God...Mel," Flynn choked the words out.

The woman's lips were curled back, teeth exposed in an unholy grin. Without taking his eyes off hers, he fumbled along the door's inner panel until his hand touched the exit sensor. He tapped it

____

and the door slid open behind him. He quickly stepped out of the room, stopping just outside of the opening. As he stood there, one hand hovering over the outer sensor pad and the other still holding and aiming the pistol, he wondered if Melanie would charge.

She didn't. She only swayed back and forth staring back at him with eyes that seemed to search for something though not able to fix its gaze. And then, in a moment that seemed to stop time, her lips closed and her eyes, which seconds before had been glassy and unfocused, locked onto his.

"Mel. Honey. Can you hear me?" Flynn asked.

Melanie didn't answer, but she didn't attack.

"Do you understand what I'm saying? Babe, are you in there?" Flynn begged.

Melanie straightened a little, the hunch less pronounced, and she stopped swaying. She blinked and seemed to try to talk. Tears ran down her face.

Flynn stepped toward her, and she took a corresponding step backward. They stayed this way, not over ten feet apart, for several moments.

Flynn's heart was in his throat, pounding with heart-wrenching agony. He wanted to reach out to her, hold her in his arms, make it all better. Then Melanie's head jerked, shifted sideways, and then cringed downwards. It was if something had reached up and pulled her head down from the inside her body, creasing and compressing it.

The swaying started again, and her eyes lost their focus. Flynn took a small step back. He lifted his pistol, which had been dangling at his side and aimed.

A low rumble emanated from Melanie's throat. A hoarse staccato growl that Flynn sensed was a warning to an attack. He shot his hand over and hit the door's sensor just as Melanie's lips curled back in an evil clown grin. She let out a roar and rushed at him. The door swiftly closed but just before it sealed, Melanie's hand slipped into the opening. The door's sensors instantly slid the core back and out of the way, a safety measure that all entries onboard possessed. Flynn shuffled jerkily back with Mel matching his steps toward him.

"Mel, no! Stop!" Flynn screamed.

She didn't, he fired.

****

"I'll make them pay," Colonel Layton Briggs sneered through gritted teeth. "Get me back to the caravan, now!" He barked at his driver. With Donnie Thompson's plea for help still ringing in his ears, Briggs decided that it was time to clear the scavengers from the area once and for all. His colony had encountered the beings on more than one occasion. However, other than a few minor scrapes, no scavenger had ever been successful in attacking his people. That had all changed.

There was no telling how many of his men survived the surprise attack, but he'd get back to his main force, gather all his weaponry, and then return and kill every scavenger he could find.

An hour later, Brigg's command vehicle emerged from a clearing and came on to the main road where he'd left his force behind a few hours earlier. "There!" Briggs said as he pointed towards the caravan's tracks heading south. "Follow those tracks and get me to my men!"

The military vehicle's engine roared, and the car jumped forward and raced southward along the tracks. Filled with potholes and broken pavement, the road was still smooth enough to navigate at a much higher rate of speed than it had while moving off road. Fifteen minutes later they came to a large clearing, and that's where the tracks going south seemed to evaporate.

"What the hell?" Layton mumbled as he scanned the road. "Stop the car," he ordered. He got out and examined the ground. "Something happened. The trucks appeared to have stopped here as the tracks go no further south. Then it looks like our men exited their vehicles for some reason. There are hundreds of boot prints everywhere. But then it looks like some of them got back into the trucks, turned the convoy around, and headed back the way they came."

Layton walked around, scratching at his chin as he went. "But see here, not everyone got back in the vehicles. There are boot tracks alongside the truck tracks."

"Do you think they were attacked by the people from Boulderside?" the driver asked.

"No, not possible. There is no way those beaten people could have caught up to us, we devastated their entire colony. And besides, they have no vehicles. No, not them, but who? And how did they attack? There isn't a single shell casing anywhere. If our troops were attacked, a hell of a battle would have ensued. Major Dominguez would have seen to that. And yet, nothing. No sign of a battle or struggle of any kind. No blood, no bodies, nothing."

"Follow me," Layton instructed his driver. With the MRAP trailing a few yards behind, Layton explored the scene. "This makes no sense," he said under his breath. "There are tracks from where the vehicles were driven to this point, and then they turned around. And here are dozens of tracks from people walking away. At one point, they appear to run. What the hell is going on?"

Layton got back into the vehicle. "Follow the tracks but go slow."

The driver put the MRAP in low gear and the vehicle crept along with the two keeping their eyes on the traffic patterns as they headed back north. After about 400 yards, the vehicle tracks continued, but many boot tracks left the roadway.

"Follow those tracks," Layton said as he pointed toward the boot traffic. The driver drove off the roadway and traced along the hundreds of boot prints in the sand. After an hour, they came upon a long line of bedraggled soldiers trudging southward. "What the hell?" Layton said as he gazed at his men. Layton tapped on his driver's shoulder, "Go around and take me to the front of the line."

The driver skirted the troops and made its way to where Major Dominguez and Sargent Hendricks were plodding along at the head of the force. The car slid to a stop in front of the two startled men.

"What the hell is going on? Where are your vehicles and weapons? And where are our captives?" Layton screamed.

<hr>

"Did you not see?" the major asked in surprise. "The Martian ship, it . . ." Dominguez hesitated and then said defiantly, "They attacked us with their insolvency ray. We could have all been wiped out. Isn't that right, sergeant?"

Hendricks immediately chimed in, "Yes, sir. It felt like my skin was going to cook right off my body. I'm telling you, if we hadn't retreated, you would have found nothing but a bunch of liquified bones laying by the road."

"What the hell are you talking about? What is an insolvent gun?"

"Insolvency *ray*, sir. They said if we didn't leave, they'd use it on us. You should have felt it. It was like having a million ants all over your body," Dominguez explained in a panic.

"And yet, here you are. Where are your weapons?"

"They are laying on the road next to the trucks," Hendricks answered, fear clearly in his voice.

"I just left that area. There was nothing there, which means the Boulderside residents have taking them."

"I'm sure it was the Martians. We never saw anyone from Boulderside."

"So, these Martians, with their huge ship, decided to take your vehicles and weapons?"

Dominguez and Hendricks looked at each other, neither wanting to be the one to answer.

"The Martians threatened to boil you, and you never fired a shot? Instead, you laid down your weapons and ran?" Layton roared, his face trembling with rage.

"Sir, their ship was huge. It moved toward us, hovering above the ground like an enormous metal monster. It blew shit all over the place. The noise was deafening, and a booming voice warned us that if we didn't drop our weapons and leave our equipment, they were going to kill us. My hair stood straight up; you should have seen it."

"But you never fired a shot?"

"I mean, uh, well no. Sir, I had to make a judgment call to save our troops. We could have all been zapped by their crazy ray."

Layton didn't hesitate, he pulled his handgun out and shot the major in the forehead. "Coward!" he said as he jammed the weapon back into its holster. "Hendricks, we're going home to re-arm ourselves, and then we'll come back and pay our respect to those Martians. After that, we will pay another visit to our friends at Boulderside.

"Yes sir!" Hendricks said followed by a swift salute. "Uh, sir?"

"What is it, *Major*,"

Hendricks swallowed hard and then, glancing back toward the end of the caravan, he said, "Where are the rest of the troops you took with you?"

Chapter 31

The laser blast hit Melanie in the left shoulder. She let out a small groan and spun sideways before dropping to one knee. Flynn, laser pistol still in hand, was crushed by what he'd done. He staggered and then braced himself against the wall. But the torturous moment hadn't passed. Melanie, head down, slowly turned back toward Flynn.

"Stay down. Mel, please, stay down," Flynn begged. But he wasn't talking to a rational person, someone who was aware of where or even who she was. The disease had taken control of Melanie's mind, and all human reason had evaporated. Her head drifted up and looked at Flynn. The snarling lips were still there.

"Mel, I will shoot you again if you don't stay down."

Moving faster than he expected, Melanie sprang up and lunged. Her fiancé' didn't hesitate. This time, the blast hit Bradshaw dead in the center of her chest. The impact of the laser, set on maximum stun, hurtled the woman backward. She landed on her back sliding a good six or seven feet across the floor. When she skidded to a stop she had come to rest back inside her quarters.

Flynn raced to her side. "My god, what have I done?" Smoke trailed up from her chest in a soft spiral. There was a burn mark in her uniform. Looking down at the woman that was his life, his reason for living, he marveled at how normal and peaceful she looked. Only thing, she didn't appear to be breathing. Her eyes were closed, and she seemed dead. "No, dear god no," Flynn stuttered as he knelt beside her.

He put his fingers on her neck to check for a pulse. He couldn't sense one. He moved his fingers, searching for any hint of a blood flow. He thought he might have felt something. With a steady stream of tears flowing down his face, he concentrated with all his senses. He choked back a sob, waiting for any sign of life. A long tense moment of excruciating anguish was interrupted when Melanie's eyes flew open. Flynn jumped up and back. *What was happening?*

Melanie moved, turning her head from side to side. Flynn watched, eyes bulging wide in shock. Suddenly, Melanie bolted upright. She stared at Flynn, that look of hunger once more apparent in her gaze. Her lips curled and a slow sinister growl emanated from her throat. She began to move, slow and deliberate, with the growl getting louder and louder. Then her teeth started rapidly chomping.

Flynn sighed, deep and with anguish—and then he tapped the code on the outer door. The panel closed, and he initiated the lock sequence. He stood outside of Melanie's quarters for several minutes, partly in shock, mostly in sadness. He could hear movement on the other side of the sealed panel. At first only a searching scratching or scraping sound, and then several loud bangs. Then nothing.

After several moments of silence, Flynn turned and headed back to the cargo bay. With each wearisome step, he re-visited what had just happened. The thoughts ate away at his heart making his legs feel like water-soaked logs. He wasn't turning, he knew that. He was simply heartbroken, and his body was fighting his every movement. He finally made it to the top of the ship's exit ramp and was about to walk down when Brad Cummings spotted him and trotted over. "Hey, how is she?" his concerned friend and pilot asked.

"Turned into one of those…things," Flynn uttered, barely above a whisper. The two men stood silent for a few moments as no words could be said by either. Finally, Flynn asked, "What's the status of the crew?"

"Of those that came down to the cargo hold, all but two were clean. Ensigns Flowers and Contreras already had trace amounts of the disease in their blood. I had a security team escort them back to their quarters and locked them in. Flynn, they were scared. Really terrified. Doc gave them a tranquilizer that will allow them to sleep. But when they asked him what would happen when they woke, if they were going to turn into one of those creatures? Well, Doc's silence made things clear.

The remaining clean crew members were ushered off the ship, and we've erected temporary housing for them, as well as a place for Dr. Carlson to work. The Doc has taken the blood we've drawn and is running tests. And, oh, roll up your sleeve."

Flynn, who had been staring vacantly at the floor since they had begun talking about Melanie, looked over at Brad. With a face that seemed to have aged ten years, he exhaled heavily and then did as requested. Cummings secured the sample and initiated the test. Had the sample been tainted with the disease, a red light would flash. If not, a green light. The two stared at the small Medilyzer. The test seemed to take an interminable time to complete. The light flashed green.

"Whew," Cummings said.

Flynn didn't openly react. Though inwardly relieved, there was a moment when he didn't care if he had the disease or not. Walking from Melanie's quarters had been traumatizing and he had begun feeling sorry for himself. Losing her was like having his heart ripped from his chest.

"We should be okay now that we've separated ourselves from the affected crew. Doc thinks that the only way the sickness could have spread so fast is through the ventilation system. It's a miracle every one of us isn't infected," Brad said.

"All I know is that Carlson better come up with a miracle or two of his own, and fast. We have no one on the ship monitoring our surroundings. We're kind sitting out here in the open, not to mention only having a limited food supply," Flynn said.

"Hadn't thought about that," Cummings said, scratching his chin as he looked up the ramp toward the ship. He did a slow turn and peered out toward the mountains. "Yeah, this isn't good."

"Let's go talk to Doc," Flynn said, and he strode toward the makeshift laboratory.

****

Traveling in a herd-like formation, a large group of humans made their way through the woods in a north-westerly direction. The man at the head of the pack walked in a somewhat upright stance and his cadence was mostly smooth and purposeful. The rest of his party moved like jerky piano metronome's, swaying back and forth as they shuffled behind him.

The group was bloodied, both from their recent battle and from feeding on the defeated victims of that battle. But they paid their disarray no heed. They simply followed their leader without thought or question of where they were going. Yet, the scavenger leader was homed in on the Boulderside colony. He'd found a few of them, attacked them but had to flee. Yet this being had an awareness that others of his ilk did not. He had their scent and remembered where they were.

Forty miles to the south, another group was trudging into their base camp. Smaller in number, this beaten and bedraggled entourage was being led by another type of human. This man was a vicious killer. An earthling with one thing on his mind, revenge.

"Hendricks," Major Briggs Layton bellowed, "You've got two hours to get your men fed, re-armed and ready to get back on the road. We'll take the three remaining vehicles with the fifty calibers, the two large cannons, and sixty more men."

Hendricks saluted and then scurried off to fulfill his duties. Layton stood surveying his camp. Speaking to no one, he said through gritted teeth, "I will make them pay. All of them."

****

"Doc," Everett said as he and Cummings walked up to the enclosed make-shift lab, "How's it going?"

"Captain," Carlson said as he looked up, he didn't answer the question, but posed one himself, "Melanie?"

Everett only shook his head.

The doc sighed and said, "Well, good and bad news here. MA and I have identified agents within the test subject's blood that we believe are causing the radical alterations we have seen," Carlson said.

"So that's good, right?" Brad Cummings said.

"It is. However, there appear to be at least two strains of this virus so far, and I believe there is at least one more strain I don't have."

"Meaning, a sample from one of the local scavengers," Everett chimed in.

"Precisely. I think the strains are different based on who passed it along. In Mr. Sanchez's situation he was apparently infected by a local pure-blood scavenger. His blood has a stronger more virulent makeup of foreign bodies in it. The blood samples from Jones, Stone, and Johnson, though almost the same, show a slight variation in the virus. But the real interesting part is how all the infections have similar qualities to our data on earth's rabies. It would explain how the disease is passed by a bite or possibly a scratch," Carlson said.

"I'm sensing a but here..."

"Yes. A big one. It is very rare for Rabies to be transmitted via air. Not impossible, but highly improbable. Therefore, a major alteration had to occur for that to happen. I'm thinking it was the nuclear element I believe Mr. Tate explained to us during our meeting. The Cranial Microcephaly Syndrome or CMS must have started due to the nuclear bombing. So, we must get a sample of a pure-blood local scavenger to really understand what we are dealing with, and to find the right antibodies to create a cure."

"Which means we must find one, capture it, and then bring it back here. And we need to do it now," Cummings said.

"I'm afraid so," the doctor said resignedly.

"We've got forty unaffected crew. Of those, less than twenty have any real training with our weaponry. We'll have to leave some here in case there are any surprises that might pop up while we're gone. We'll take two of the remaining drones, leave two, and half of the hand-held weapons. Brad, see to it. Have Ms. Grant choose who will go with us, and who will stay. Round up the arms we will need and a day's rations and meet me back here in twenty minutes," Everett instructed.

Cummings turned on his heels and sped off. M.A. stood up and moved to Everett's side.

"Where are you going?" Everett asked.

"With you of course. You'll need me to help you capture the cursed being. After all, if I am bitten, I can't get infected," the droid said.

"M.A., I'm sure the Doc needs you here to finish up with what you've been doing.

"Actually, without the local subject, we are almost done here. I must agree with M.A," Doc Carlson said.

Everett thought of Melanie. Taking M.A. with him leaves her here unprotected. He grimaced and then nodded. Fifteen minutes later, seventeen crewmen including Brad Cummings and Marc Antony, stood at the shield, armed and ready.

"Have you scanned the area?" Everett said to M.A.

"Yes sir. There is quite a large contingency of humans here," the droid said as he pointed to a spot on his info-pad. "They are not the colonists. The problem is this group appears to be heading right towards the Boulderside settlement."

"How long before they reach them?"

"They are not moving fast. At their current rate, and if they don't stop, about two hours," M.A. said.

"If we leave now, and move at our top speed, where would we come into contact with them?"

M.A. did a few calculations. "We could easily reach their flank at this point in Forty-three minutes," he said as he pointed again at his info-pad.

"Ok. And if we go straight to Boulderside?"

"Nineteen minutes."

Everett thought for a moment. Every minute counted if he was to help his crew beat the virus before it was too late. The problem was, he only intended on grabbing a contaminated scavenger from the rear of their faction and then race back, hopefully, undetected by the rest of the flesh-eaters. However, if he did that and didn't warn the Boulderside residents of the impending horde heading their way, there could be another slaughter of the inhabitants. And this time, they wouldn't survive.

"Ok. We'll go to Boulderside and inform them of the scavengers heading their way. With the advanced warning and proper preparations, and with the weaponry they now possess, they should easily be able to protect themselves," Everett said. "M.A., plot a course and lead the way."

The droid looked at his info-pad, dialed in the coordinates, memorized them, and then nodded at Everett. "We'll follow you," Everett said.

Chapter 32

Moving slowly but tenaciously, a grunting growling band of carnivorous beings was moving to a destination that only their leader knew they were going. Yet, none of the multitudes behind him gave any indication of approval or disapproval. And though the plodding man had no map or device telling him where to go or how much farther they needed to travel, he knew they would soon arrive at that destination. Like a shark that can sense blood in the water from vast distances, he knew.

Several miles to the southwest, a smaller party moved at an incredible speed, heading to the same destination. They were led by an eight-foot man that moved with the speed and agility of an African gazelle. His entire team showed little outward emotion seemingly focused and steadfast in their determination. Guiding this throng was a device so modern and futuristic, that mere thought waves were all that was needed to follow the proper coordinates.

Six miles to his group's southwest was one more assemblage converging on the same destination. This band of marauders, well over 200 strong, was hellbent on destruction. Led by a killer with revenge on his mind, the military man had worked his men up into a frenzy and they were frothing at the mouth to kill. They knew where they were going due to a disloyal prior resident who'd given up the destination to these killers for power and sexual domination.

Three groups, all headed for a fateful meeting that could only leave death and destruction in their wake. The first to arrive made their trek in just under nineteen minutes. Barely breathing hard though controlled, Captain Flynn Everett and his team strode up to the Boulderside colony. Larry Tate, and a small number of his encampment, were there using one of the vehicles they had confiscated to haul some of their dead from the earlier attack for burial.

"What's happened?" Tate asked, "Why are ya here?"

"Scavengers, heading this way. A lot of them. You need to set up a perimeter firing position with barricades along that small ridge," Everett said as he surveyed the hillside. "With the weapons you now possess, you should easily be…"

"Captain?" M.A. interrupted.

"M.A.?"

"We have another problem. There is a different group of around 175 humans heading this way. This contingent is coming from the southwest. I believe they are the forces we dealt with earlier."

"You have got to be kidding," Everett said.

"No sir, I'm not," M.A. said surprised.

Everett ignored M.A.'s misunderstanding of his comment's meaning and turned to the colony leader. "Mr. Tate, it looks like we are going to have to stand together and fight."

"Fight? Captain, my people exhausted. We wouldn't stand a chance. Couldn't yar ship come and set up that energy shield that we could get behind? No one could get to us then. Could they? Then we wouldn't hafta fight."

"No, they couldn't. However, I'm afraid that's not possible now. Much of our crew that is needed to operate the ship are infected and confined to their quarters. Those that are not infected are outside of the ship in makeshift lodgings or here with me now. Until we get this infection under control, the ship must stay where it is."

Everett looked around, remembered the size of the colony, and came to another tough conclusion. "And, at this point, we do not have enough time to gather up your people and move them within the ship's shield perimeter even if we wanted to. If we are encountered while in transit, which seems very likely, we would be in an open space which would be very difficult to defend without significant loss of life. No, we need the height advantage that you have here."

Moving to his left, he pointed and said, "the enemy will have to scale the mountain, which will expose them to our fire above. We can set up flanking positions with our drones for their firepower and reconnaissance visuals, and if we can get the military vehicles you now have to that flat section about thirty meters up, we will be able to cover incursions from most any direction."

"Very well. But I must tell ya, my people are already a beaten-up bunch. And none of them have ever fired the kinds of weapons we now possess," Tate professed.

"Understood. Yet, our alternatives are few and I believe the survival of all of us depends on our ability to defend your colony. Let's get to it."

Preparations, as best as they could be done, went forward with all able-bodied men and a few women from the colony going about the chore of arranging protection and setting up their defenses.

With the help of the Martian team, what would have taken half a day took barely more than an hour. And their timing couldn't have been better.

"Captain?" M.A. said as he studied the info-pad.

"Which group?" Everett asked, knowing what the droid was alerting him to.

"All. And what I mean by all is that the military force has broken into three groups. They are coming at us in a pronged approach. A group of about forty men is circling from the west, with another group of the same size moving toward the east. The rest of the men, around 120, are shifting toward the center of the colony's main entrance. At the same time, the scavengers are coming as one faction from the east."

"Well, this could be rather interesting. Let's put the bulk of our defenses in a position to meet the main military force from the middle, with the healthiest colonists on our right flank with drone number one. We'll let the scavengers and drone number two handle our left flank." At that moment, there was a shriek, and then another and another until it was a crescendo of wailing. The east flanking forces of the scavengers and militia had found one another.

****

"Scavengers?" Major Briggs Layton scoffed. "Perfect. Now we won't have to go searching for those rotting bastards later. We'll take them out too, here, and now. Then, once we've retrieved all our weaponry from the soon-to-be slaughtered residents of this stinking mountain, we'll find those Martians and take their ship. Oh, this is going to be a good day. A very good day, indeed. Hendricks, sound the attack."

Now a second lieutenant, Buddy Hendricks began turning the handle of an age-old air raid siren alerting their troops to begin the assault. Briggs, like the generals of old, stayed back well out of harm's way. He lit a wretched smelling cigar and sat back in the front of the fully enclosed MRAP, fully expecting that the battle would be over in short order. He quickly heard gunfire, a single shot, and then automatic weapons. He began to chuckle, a laugh of a tyrant, and then blew out a big puff of smoke.

Everett surveyed electronic imagery sent to his info-pad by the drones. The battle between the enemy troops and the scavengers to the east was quickly becoming a route. There were just too many scavengers. Every time one went down to gunfire, another one, or two, or three took his place. Drone number two, hovering above the melee, had been held back from firing, but now Everett instructed the device to move toward the rear of the scavenger pack and attack.

To maim or kill, the drone had to fire using full power. At this output, the drones needed time to regenerate after ten full-power shots. There was only a short delay, no more than ten seconds, but during this time, they were vulnerable.

There were easily 150 scavengers when they met the forty militiamen. Twenty minutes into the battle, thirty scavengers lay dead with nearly twenty-five militia deceased and being eaten. The other fifteen men had retreated toward Brigg's position.

When the attack alert was sounded, the center militia attack force had raced toward the mountain like Viking marauders. They were whooping and hollering hell-bent on destruction and mayhem while expecting only minimal resistance. Briggs believed the colonist would be in the mountain recuperating from the earlier raid, with little anticipation of their return.

The major had instructed his troops to scream bloody murder, as they had in the earlier raid, expecting that many inside the colony would drop their weapons and try to escape from the rear emergency exit. The colonists had done this before, and there was no reason to think that they weren't stupid enough to try it again. That's why his west flanking troops were sent there. They would be waiting in ambush. *Like shooting fish in a barrel, as his mother used to say.*

The first laser blast shocked those that saw it and had them staggering back in terror. It was a lightning streak of blue that blasted into its victim, killing him instantly. A blink later, and a half dozen more flashes shot down from above. These laser beams killed three more before anyone could comprehend what was happening. At the same time, the sounds of fifty-caliber machine guns and other gunfire rang out as the colonists opened fire with the weaponry they had secured from the last raids. Nothing could have been more astonishing to the invaders. Instead of experiencing little or no resistance, they were instead being met with a hail of bullets and strange killer laser beams.

Within minutes, all the militia's vehicles were out of action with two blowing up from hits to their gas tanks, and a third crashing into a tree when a fifty-caliber bullet ripped the driver's head off. Briggs heard the explosions but wasn't sure what they were from. He was confused. Suddenly, a face exploded into the side window of his car. It bore a gnarling pale and diseased devil's smile, teeth chomping, chin and cheeks covered by a bloody mixture of red and green goo. The thing was clawing with ravaged fingers trying to get in.

Chapter 33

"Why haven't we seen anyone trying to leave yet? Once the shooting started last time, we had already captured fifteen women and killed ten or so men," a militiaman said from the west emergency escape exit of the colony.

"Maybe they aren't as dumb as Briggs thought they were."

"Yeah, maybe. He's not so bright neither." They both chuckled.

"Hey, what's that?" the first soldier said as he pointed toward the sky. One of the spaceship's drones had slid down from its elevated station to around fifty feet above the hidden soldiers.

"Not sure, but let's shoot it," The other said. He took aim and was about to squeeze off a shot when a blazing blue streak of light shot from the sphere and struck him in the eye he was aiming with. The laser beam bore a hole through his head, killing him instantaneously.

"What the…" the other soldier started to say when a second beam of light shot him in the temple. The drone had identified all the men on the west side of the mountain, designed a firing sequence, and began picking them off one by one. Five men lay dead before the man in command of these troops, Sergeant Anthony "Tank" Rizzoli, saw the sphere and ordered those remaining to open fire. When they did, a barrage of bullets from the colonists hidden above them began raining down.

M.A. had used the sphere to bring the militia out of their hiding. They were so overtaken by the device and their desire to hit the hovering craft, that they left themselves vulnerable. Seven more died from the drone and eleven others lay dead from the colonist fusillade before they knew what hit them. The entire engagement lasted all of three minutes.

Those scavengers not feeding on the dead militia from the colonist's east flank had followed Brigg's men back to the main militia force. The attacking military men were now being counter-attacked from all sides. The main force that had been racing up the face of the mountain, certain they would overcome any opposition, were now retreating in full run.

As these men rushed back, bullets and laser blasts were pinging and thudding all around. The retreat was an unorganized melee of withdrawing men. The problem was, they were running right at over 100 scavengers, and the Martians and colonists knew it.

"Though I believe the outcome of this battle is going to go down to the last combatant below us, we need one of those scavengers alive. M.A., where is the east flanking drone?" Everett asked when there was a break in the firing from the colonist's defensive position. M.A. tapped his info-pad screen and then watched the drone's camera.

"It is hovering near the rear of the pack," M.A. said. The droid looked to the captain for instructions when he saw Everett's left shoulder fly back and he staggered backward. M.A. rushed to his side. There was blood flowing freely from a large gunshot wound. "Captain, you have been hit."

"No kidding? Don't answer that," Everett said weakly.

Larry Tate moved over and quickly examined the wound. "Bullet went clean through. You should be ok, but we'll need to stop that bleedin'."

Several first aid stations were set up along the defensive perimeter. Betty Davidson, a colonist of around forty, came over. "You'll have to get to a knee so I can work on that," she said as she stared up at the towering Martian. Even on her tiptoes, she would have had a difficult time reaching the area that needed tending to. Everett dropped down and Davidson went to work.

The colonists didn't have much in the way of medicines, mostly herbs and homemade tonics and poultices. Davidson, all of five-feet-two, packed the holes with a brown compound that looked a lot like chewed up tobacco, and then took clean rags and pressed it on both the entrance and exit wound locations. She then had M.A. wrap the shoulder. The woman looked like a child working on an adult twice her size. But she was forceful and efficient in her work.

"M.A. You're going to have to take charge. Have the surveillance drones continue an all-out assault on all fronts. But remember, we need at least one of the scavengers alive."

"Yes sir," M.A. said, and then he began tapping rapidly on his info-pad.

※※※※※

"My God!" Major Briggs cried out. He shrank back away from the window in terror. His cigar, which had been firmly and arrogantly planted in the corner of his mouth, drooped, and then fell to the floor. "You idiot. Get us the hell out of here," he yelled at his man. The panicked driver started the car, put the vehicle in drive, and jammed down on the accelerator. But it was too late. The vehicle was surrounded by dozens of scavengers that made no effort to move out of the way when the car advanced.

Though the car jumped forward, the bodies quickly piled up causing the vehicle to bounce up into the air and lurch sideways. When the wheels came down it shot the car hard to the right initiating a violent impact into a tree. The collision caused the front windshield to dislodge from its frame. The glass panel didn't fall out, it just opened just enough for fingers to creep in.

Briggs had been thrown around inside the car as it bounced and careened, hitting his head hard on the ceiling several times and then smashing his face into the side window. He was dazed and disoriented for several seconds and closed his eyes in pain. When he finally felt like his head had stopped spinning, he opened his eyes. What he saw caused a jolt of terror to explode through his entire being. The car was completely covered and surrounded by scavengers. They were clawing and pawing at the vehicle, banging, and slapping at it. Doing all their feeble minds could instruct to get in.

"Reverse, reverse. Damn it, put the car in reverse and get us out of here," Briggs demanded. His driver didn't respond. A trickle of blood flowed from a large gash in his forehead. He was breathing, but unconscious. Briggs spun his head from side to side and then looked out the rear window, hoping for a way to escape. But all he saw were the faces of mouth-chomping scavengers desperate to find a way to get in.

With no way to flee, Briggs lunged forward toward the driver's seat. He would get the MRAP started and get them out of there. He placed his hands on his driver's shoulders and was about to wrench him out of the way when the scavengers on the hood of the car slid off and moved away. Briggs stared out and saw a man climbing on the hood. He was a scavenger, but he seemed less ravaged than the others. Briggs watched as he made his way to the windshield and then locked his fingers in the opening caused by the wreck and began to pull.

Briggs' eyes bulged as he realized what was happening. Never, in all the stories had he been told of a scavenger making this kind of a mental effort. He re-doubled his frantic efforts to get the driver out of his seat. Briggs was a big man, not in great shape, but still strong. He used every ounce of his strength to pull the driver out of his seat and push him out of the way. Just as he lifted his leg to climb into the front, the windshield pulled away exposing him to the outside.

Slamming back into his seat, Briggs pulled his revolver out and began firing into the now attacking throng. Though he hit several, none of his shots were killing shots and those climbing in kept coming. After emptying his first ammo clip, he reached into his ammo belt and pulled out another. Before he could even get the clip in four scavengers were working their way simultaneously through the now open windshield.

Briggs gasped and shoved the new clip in his gun. This time, he made three immediate kills as he shot each attacker in the head. Those scavengers fell limp in the opening, bodies half in, half out. The next shot from Briggs grazed the fourth scavenger's temple and lodged in his shoulder. But the injury barely slowed his egress as he continued climbing in, mouth chomping and clanking in wild abandon. Other

———————

scavengers were now endeavoring to climb in over their dead comrades. There was no sense of organization as they practically brawled with each other to get through the tight aperture.

The big military man let out a small scream of panic and began booting the scraggly wounded attacker in its head while focusing on two more scavengers now climbing in and over their dead comrades. Sounding like a kicked dog, Briggs let out a squeal and pulled off three more shots killing those two. Now the window opening was clogged with dead scavengers like a can of packed sardines The beasts had been so avid at getting to Briggs, they had wedged themselves in where it became impossible for others to follow.

The last scavenger still alive inside the car pulled on the seats with his hands and kicked with his feet to get at Briggs. The soldier fired 2 more shots, but because the scavenger was wriggling madly to get in, he only winged the thing in the shoulder grazed the top of his back.

Realizing he would need to save his ammunition when he got out of the car, he pulled out his large knife and began hacking at the scavenger's clawing hands and arms. He looked for an opening and waited till he could get a good kill angle. He finally got it and from underneath shoved the knife into his assailant's neck and up into its brain. The scavenger went limp.

Briggs had won the battle and came out of it without a scratch. He had almost been eaten by these fiends but got the better of them. He was the winner, again. He was sweating profusely and felt a stream run down his face and into his eyes. He wiped it away with his sleeve. When he did, he happened a glance at his uniform and saw that it was covered with a reddish-green syrupy fluid. He gasped and began feverishly wiping at his face with his hands. When he pulled them away, they were covered with the thick fluid.

Now in a complete state of horror, Briggs began screaming for someone to get him out. His pleas, however, only fell on those who couldn't understand and only wanted to eat him.

Above this scene, some 100 meters away, the team of Martians and Boulderside residents continued to fire away at any moving target they could see. Most of the militia had run off like fleeing rats from a fire. Those still lingering were quickly dispatched by the hovering drones that used infrared sighting to weed out any in hiding.

"We've got to send out a team to catch one of the scavengers," Everett said to M.A. "We can't let the retreating militia below kill them all or let them escape off into the woods forcing us to waste time tracking them down and capturing them."

"Yes Captain," M.A. agreed. The android gathered four Martians together and explained their mission. With Everett wounded, chief Security officer Belinda Grant would lead the team. After a few moments of preparation, they acknowledged the importance of their task to the captain and headed out. Everett stayed behind with Tate and the other colonists. Miraculously, the only injury by the defenders of the mountain was to Everett. No Boulderside resident received even a nick.

"How are you feelin'?" Tate asked Flynn.

"I've been better, though I thought I'd have more pain. The salve seems to be quite effective."

"Yes, it is quite remarkable. Captain, if'n yar doin' ok, I'm gonna to go inside to give the colony an update. I'm sure by now they are goin' a bit crazy," Tate said. Everett nodded his approval. After Tate moved off, Everett walked down the lines of defense toward their left flank. He checked those Boulderside defenders, verifying their condition and congratulating them on rebuffing the advancing army.

After confirming that all was well, he made his way back to the east side of the mountain. This area had the smallest amount of Boulderside residents. He passed the last guard and then went down and around the trail toward a steep embankment. It was due to this sharp incline that less defenders were needed. Being careful not to slip, he made his way almost to the bottom. He could see many dead scavengers and at least twenty to twenty-five dead militiamen. There were other bodies of scavengers strewn about leading to the right and towards the military force's main battery.

Seeing that all was calm here, Everett turned to head back up the embankment when he glimpsed movement from his right. In the trees, about fifteen meters away, a figure moved.

"Who's there? Come out," Everett demanded, laser pistol drawn.

There was no answer, but Everett could see that someone was moving toward his position. He pulled back to a level spot, setting his feet, and preparing to fire if necessary. The foliage was thick here, and except for a glimpse or two as the person headed his way, he couldn't tell who it was, though he felt certain it wasn't one of his crew.

"Be aware that I have my laser pistol set on kill and I won't hesitate to shoot." Everett was direct and sincere with his demand.

But still, there was no response. A hand sifted its way through the bushes and separated several branches to allow whoever it was to pass through. Everett raised his pistol to fire. The apparent leader of the scavengers stepped through.

"Well, I certainly didn't expect it to be you," Flynn said as his hand tensed around his weapon. The scavenger didn't speak, only stared at the much larger man. "Can you speak or communicate in any way?" The cannibal didn't reply only tilted his head slightly. After a moment of silence, he opened his mouth as if to talk, but only a few groans and moans came out.

Taking a small step forward, Everett lowered his pistol and nodded his head toward the man. "I'd like to be able to communicate, not kill each other. Is that possible? Can you understand what I am trying to suggest?"

The scavenger's head moved very slightly up and down. Everett wasn't sure if he was acknowledging him or mimicking his earlier movement. "I know this is going to sound crazy, but I'd like to take you back to my ship, do some tests on you. We're looking for a cure and you might be the answer to help us and your kind. Will you do that? Will you come back with me?"

The scavenger only stared, but Everett thought he noticed contemplation in his eyes. Putting his pistol in its holster, Everett raised his good arm, hand out in a calming manner. "I'm not really sure how we're going to do this, but if you understand what I'm saying, I'm going to move back up to the encampment above. I'd like you to follow me. Once there, I'll arrange to have us transported to the ship,"

Everett said. He used his hand and motioned the being to follow him up the mountain.

After moving five or so steps, he saw that the scavenger wasn't following. He raised his hand again indicating to him to follow. It was then that the man grunted several times and five scavengers burst from the bushes and raced toward Everett. He quickly pivoted but lost his balance on the steep incline and fell. He turned his body in the air just in time not to land on his hurt shoulder but in doing so landed flat on his back.

With the five beings only a few feet away, Everett pulled out his pistol and fired. He hit two but knew he wouldn't have enough time to shoot the other three before they would be on him. He raised up and tried to get to his feet. He was much bigger and stronger, but he was hurt and that would even the odds of him being able to defend himself without being bitten or scratched. Just as the next two scavengers were about to pounce, M.A. came crashing out of the bush from his right and leveled the two attackers. Behind him came several other of the Martian team.

The scavenger leader, as he had done several times before, turned to flee. But this time, three Martians, led by Lieutenant Grant, were there. The three, with pistols set on full stun, each shot, and the man went down in a heap. The last scavenger still standing, now less than five feet away from Everett, seemed at a loss on what to do, where to go, or whom to try to eat. He didn't get the chance to decide. One of Everett's crew, with laser on full kill, blasted the scavenger with a blue laser beam to the temple.

"Well, talk about good timing. Thanks, M.A., for saving my butt. I was in a bit of a bind," Everett said.

"We came back to let you know we had a captive. But when you weren't there, we came looking for you," Grant said.

"Good thing, or I'd probably would have been a Big Mac for these guys" Everett said. M.A. looked at him for a moment in confusion. "It was an old Earth sandwich from...never mind. Let's take the leader with us along with the one you have. Doc may want to take a closer look at him since he seems to be a bit more human than the rest. What's the status of the rest of the scavengers and the invading military?"

"Mostly routed by each other. Our drones wiped out any scavenger still left except these five here and the one we captured. The militia, what's left of them, have all fled. I have one of the drones tracking them," Grant said.

"Good, let's get to Tate, let them know the status of things, and then get back to the ship. To make the trip as fast as possible, we'll take one of the captured trucks. M.A., do you think you could drive one of those things?" The droid stared at him as if his captain had lost every brain cell. "Ok, you'll drive then," Everett said knowing the android's brain would quickly assimilate to the functions of the truck.

Chapter 34

It took longer to truss and secure the scavengers and load them in the truck than it did to drive the ten miles or so to get back to the ship. M.A. did an adequate job driving, though not without a few scares along the way.

When they arrived, Doc Carlson greeted them with news. "I've isolated the neural inhibitors from the infection that has affected the crew. With samples from the original hosts, I am fairly certain I can come up with a vaccine that will prevent any more of us from getting it."

"A preventative? What about the ones that already have it?" Everett asked.

"Well, it may or may not reverse the symptoms. I won't know for sure until I produce the serum and then inject it into one of the infected."

How long will this take?"

"Shouldn't take long, now that you have an indigenous host."

"Then, let's get to it," Everett said as he motioned for M.A. and Grant to bring the captives to Carlson's lab. "This one's a little different," Everett said about the purported leader they captured. "He seems to have an awareness the others don't. Not sure if that will mean anything or not."

"I'll check the blood of all of them," Carlson said as he began setting up the Medi-scanner. The scavengers were lucid but completely unable to cope with what was happening to them. Being bound up and gagged had them in a constant state of agitation, all except the leader. He moved as guided and resisted little. Once Grant and M.A. had the six men in a secured holding area, Doc Carlson pulled samples from each.

Twenty minutes later, with much of the crew standing by and watching, the Medi-scanner had identified the culprit. A mutated virus, similar to zoonoses, that appeared to be the result of a radioactive alteration. The virus virtually shut down and eliminated the brain's ability to use reason and morality.

"As I see it, the earthlings that were born as scavengers cannot be cured. The area of the brain the disease has affected in those people has been permanently eradicated. However, as I said, I should be able to produce a vaccine that will stop anyone from getting the virus again, whether they are bitten, or in the case of our crew, it is breathed in," Carlson explained to Everett.

"But we still don't know if the recently affected can be cured?" Everett asked.

"No. Again, the only way to find out is to give them the vaccine and hope."

Everett thought about this for a moment, and then said, "Can you produce a sleeping agent we can send through the ventilation system of the ship? It will be virtually impossible to inject the crew without someone getting hurt if they aren't subdued in some way."

"Yes, I can do that. It will take about half an hour for the centrifuge modulator to make the vaccine. While that is running, I will have a canister filled with a gas agent that will put everyone out. We can insert it into a ventilator valve in the loading bay shaft. It will take about fifteen minutes to run throughout the entire ship," the Doctor said as he began dialing into the Medilyzer a cocktail of potent sleeping gases.

****

"Where to first?" Carlson asked, though he was certain where Flynn was headed.

"Mel's quarters," Everett answered as expected.

Walking behind the captain and the doctor, Brad Cummings said, "Are you sure you want to use it on her first? I mean, what if it doesn't work?"

"Won't matter whom we try it on then. It's either going to work or it's not."

"Good point," Cummings said. "Well, what about a bad side effect? Then what?"

Everett slowed, considered the thought, and said, "Mel would want to be first. She wouldn't want someone else being adversely affected. If there is a side-effect then Doc will use Mel as the patient to solve whatever might occur."

"What about Sanchez? After all, he started this whole thing. If it's going to kill, maim, or screw someone up, let it be him," Cummings said, and he wasn't kidding.

Carlson looked away as Everett considered this. "Hmmm…" Three minutes later, they showed up in front of Melanie's room. Everett punched in the security override code and the door slid open. Melanie was on the floor just inside the door. Flynn dashed to her side and checked her breathing and pulse. She was still alive, thank God. Her face and the skin on her hands and forearms appeared to have sores and welts all over them. They were not open wounds, but raw-looking blotches.

"Brad, help me get her up," Carlson said as he turned Melanie on her back. Everett's arm was still in a sling so the two gently lifted the unconscious woman and placed her on the couch. Taking the injector to her neck Doc Carlson pulled the trigger, and a pre-arranged dosage of serum was injected.

"How long will it take?" Cummings asked.

"No way to be sure. I doubt the serum will act as fast as the disease did when it took over her brain, but I really can't predict." The three men stood back and watched, but nothing happened. Melanie simply slept, her breathing strong and regular. "Until we know the effectiveness of the serum, we really can't take a chance of injecting anyone else," Carlson said to Everett.

"How long will the crew stay sleeping from the gases?" Cummings asked Carlson.

"Easily twelve hours. We could also send another dosage through the air system if need be," Carlson replied.

"Can you give Melanie something that will wake her now?" Everett asked the Doc.

"Well, yes, of course. But the antidote may not work that fast. She could wake up and still be a scavenger."

"Yes, I know. But I do not feel we can wait twelve hours to see if the cure works," Everett explained. "Brad, we'll need something to hold her down, just in case." Cummings nodded and dashed out of

Melanie's quarters. Carlson took the sleeping woman's vitals again, and when he did, he tilted his head and frowned.

"What is it?" Everett said as he moved closer.

"Her blood pressure has elevated, and her pulse is racing. Not totally unexpected, but…"

"But what. Is she having an adverse reaction?"

"I'm not sure," Carlson said as he examined a few more readings on the Medilyzer. At that moment, Melanie's body went rigid, and she began to thrash around on the couch.

"What's happening Doc?" Everett blurted. Though he knew Carlson was at just as much of a loss to explain Melanie's actions as he was. Melanie's back arched and she let out a long moan before collapsing back down. She lay still for several moments, long enough for Carlson to check her again.

"Her vitals are returning to normal. I think she's alright now."

"Cured?" Everett asked in elation.

"No, I didn't mean that. Just no longer under stress. Let's see how she is when we wake her," Carlson said, trying to sound positive.

A few minutes later Cummings returned with several plastic bindings. He and Carlson wound the bindings around Melanie's feet and hands, and then secured those bindings with two more, connecting them to the couch's railing. "That should do it," Brad said.

"Are you sure you want to try this?" Carlson said as he arranged the proper medication to wake Melanie.

"We have to. We need to know if this is going to work. If it doesn't, well, I don't even want to think about that," Everett said.

Carlson's shoulder's rose and fell slightly as he put the injector next to Melanie's neck once again. He pulled the trigger and then stood and moved back several steps. After a time that seemed to take an eternity but was less than thirty seconds, Melanie stirred, if only slightly. Her eyes moved back and forth a few times under their lids and then fluttered open. Everett, Carlson, and Cummings stood transfixed, unsure of what she would do.

At first, the woman did nothing, only lay there staring up at the ceiling. Everett's heart was in his throat, and he desperately wanted to go to Mel's side. He took a step her way when Carlson grabbed his arm and stopped him. Shaking his head and holding his finger up, he whispered, "Gently call out her name. Let's see how she responds."

"Mel, it's me, Flynn. Can you hear me?" Everett said. The woman seemed not to hear or understand. He called out her name again. This time her head tilted back slightly. She sniffed the air, taking in three or four deep inhales. A low guttural growl came from her throat and then she slowly turned her head in his direction.

"It didn't work Doc," Everett said desperately.

"Like I said, it may be too soon. Let's give it time." Carlson said.

Rising into a sitting position, Melanie looked at her feet and hands. The bindings gave her just enough leeway to allow her to get in this position, but no further. She tugged on the straps a couple of times and then raised her head back up toward the three men. A snarl crossed her lips, and she began to growl. Her eyes still had the green hue to them, and she began to sway a little back and forth.

"Melanie, honey, it's me, Flynn. Can you hear me?" Everett tried. But the women didn't respond. Suddenly, she tried to jump at the men. The restraining straps kept her in place, but she was straining mightily while growling and groaning, giving her all to get at them. Her mouth began chomping up and down. She was still a scavenger, doing all she could to feed.

"My God. What are we going to do," Cummings said? Everett was thinking the same thing and both men were now looking at the Doctor.

"Captain, as I warned you, the serum I made may only be a vaccine that will prevent others from getting the disease. It may not help those that already have it. But saying that, I still think we need to give it more time," Carlson said.

Melanie was now thrashing about wildly. Carlson looked at her and then at Everett. "I think it would be best if we put her back to sleep for a while, so she doesn't hurt herself. It will also give the medicine more time to work. We can try again in a couple of hours."

"Ok. Brad and I will grab her so you can inject her," Everett said. "Brad, you go to her left, I'll go to her right. That way I can use my good arm to help you hold her. Cummings nodded and then the two started toward Melanie. The woman saw them coming at her and shrank back down onto the couch. She stopped chomping her teeth, and her growl turned to a low guttural noise.

She was staring at Everett–right at him. It was a deeply concentrated gaze. The action momentarily startled Everett causing him to pull up. Melanie closed her eyes, squeezing them tight in an action that almost seemed to cause her pain. She then began blinking, rapidly.

"What's going on doc?" Everett asked.

"I'm not sure," Carlson said. He was going to send the Medilyzer over and have it scan Melanie to see what might be happening, when she lifted her bound hands up in front of her face, palms out, in what appeared to be a defensive gesture. Her head started to move back and forth and then in a rounding effort like she was trying to crack her neck. When she lowered her hands, she was once again staring at Everett, but now, her eyes were mostly clear of the green film.

"Doc, her eyes. Look at her eyes. The green film is gone," Everett exclaimed. The snarl was also now gone, as was the slight swaying action. "Melanie, honey, can you hear me? Mel do you understand what I'm saying?"

Melanie continued to stare for several long moments. Then, her head tilted to one side, and then to the other. She seemed to be examining Everett. "Flynn?" Melanie croaked. "Flynn? What's happening?" the woman asked. Her voice was raspy, dry, and brittle sounding.

"Oh Mel," Flynn cried out and raced to her side. "Mel, thank God, oh thank God, your back," Flynn said, his voice cracking with emotion.

"What's happened? I feel so strange—and one of us really stinks," she said. The three men all laughed.

"Honey, I'm afraid that's you," Everett said still chuckling. "Mel, you were infected. For the last several days, you and more than half of our crew have been locked in your rooms. But thank God, the Doc found a cure."

Chapter 35

Over the next several hours, Doc Carlson injected the remaining crew members with the antidote. All responded well, even Gary Sanchez, though several other injuries he had endured required other attention. His broken wrist would never be the same, even after surgery.

The six indigenous scavengers also responded to the medicine, but their transformation and recuperation process took days not hours. And even then, their intellect was little more than that of a child. These people would have to be trained and taught to do the most basic of human activities and civilities. Their leader, for whatever reason, was much brighter and seemed to learn at an accelerated pace to the others. Once the six scavengers were treated with the antidote and lost their cannibalistic desires, their overall health improved. Their skin cleared and their hair grew in.

Yet, with all these accomplishments, there remained two very important situations to resolve. The first would be an investigation into the fertility issues within the non-infected human females. This would take time and much research. The second; how to help the rest of the planet's population, both scavenger and non-infected. These would be problems that Everett believed needed the expertise of other Martians.

After communicating all that had happened back to Mars, it was decided that Everett and his crew would return to Mars so that their ship could be re-stocked with additional medical and research equipment and personnel. A few members of the high Council would also join the return trip so that a base could be established for ongoing relationship building.

When the day came to return to Mars, Doc Carlson and two of his staff decided to stay behind to continue working on Earth's issues. Two scientists, a biologist and botanist, an engineer, and three security guards also stayed. The crew moved the Doc's makeshift lab to Boulderside as well as quarters for them to live. One of the ship's drones was left too, along with extra provisions and communication equipment. A high-energy solar-generated power supply was set up along with lighting equipment and other power-operated gear.

Everett offered to let Tate return with them, but he wouldn't leave his colony. Five other Boulderside residents were selected and were given quarters on the ship. With the promise to return as fast as possible, the Martians said their goodbyes, and the large spacecraft rumbled to life before lifting off and rocketing skyward. It was an awe-inspiring sight.

The trip back to Mars was uneventful. Gary Sanchez remained confined to his quarters for most of the flight and would be permanently banned from any future journeys back to Earth once his story was told to the council. The return trip was scheduled with many new faces selected to go. However, Everett would remain the captain, with most of his senior staff staying on, including Melanie and Brad Cummings. Even M.A. was pegged to return.

Communications with Carlson and the Earth team went on as scheduled with the Doctor confiding to the Martian council that he had identified several issues with the infertility problem. Nutrition was a key factor, but he also found an abnormality when he did a gene scan on several women. Additional equipment was needed to continue his research into the problem he was assured it would be added to the shipping manifest.

One Mars month later, the second Earth-bound mission left Mars. When they arrived, some seventy-two days later, they once again found Earth an inhospitable place, this time for far different reasons…THE END.

Thanks for reading and I hope you enjoyed. Please look for my other works:

The Barilla Chronicles – The Joseph Campanella Journey

Severed Ties – A Nick Cooper Story

The Lost Coast – The Revenge of Mad River Billy

www.ingramcontent.com/pod-product-compliance
Lightning Source LLC
Chambersburg PA
CBHW060343310726
48976CB00003B/708